The Christmas Carol

A Jayne Sinclair Genealogical Mystery

M. J. Lee

About M. J. Lee

Martin Lee is the author of contemporary and historical crime novels. *The Christmas Carol* is the eighth book featuring genealogical investigator, Jayne Sinclair.

The Jayne Sinclair Series

The Irish Inheritance

The Somme Legacy

The American Candidate

The Vanished Child

The Lost Christmas

The Sinclair Betrayal

The Merchant's Daughter

The Christmas Carol

The Inspector Danilov Series

Death in Shanghai

City of Shadows

The Murder Game

The Killing Time

The Inspector Thomas Ridpath thrillers

Where the Truth Lies

Where the Dead Fall

Where the Silence Calls

Where the Innocent Die

When the Past Kills

Copyright © 2018 M J Lee
All rights reserved.
ISBN-9798557351157

This book is dedicated to all those
Mancunians who laboured long and hard
in the cotton mills of the city.
Your legacy is everywhere.

PROLOGUE

December 19, 1843
Devonshire Terrace, London

Charles Dickens sat at his desk, the pile of new books stacked in front of him.

He had laboured hard on this novella, working in a frenzied fashion during the day and often taking long walks all over London at night. It was quickly written; less than six weeks from start to the final words of any author, even one as celebrated as him.

The End.

And now the novel was typeset, illustrated, printed and bound and published.

He picked up one of the copies, admiring the gold stamping on the cover with his own name and the title surrounded by a gold wreath.

He had been involved in every step of the process. Choosing the illustrator, John Leech, making sure he understood exactly what was expected. Overseeing the entire publishing process from selection of the paper and type, down to the hue of the gilt on the edge of the paper.

His publishers, Chapman & Hall, had been less than supportive, even having the temerity to ask him to pay for the cost of publication.

What had they done?

Nothing but carp about costs and the failure of his latest serial, Martin Chuzzlewit.

Never mind, at least now all the profits would go to him. He was sure it would do well; the first reviews had been laudatory. Even Thackeray had sent him his review:

'Who can listen to objections regarding such a book as this? It seems to me a national benefit, and to every man or woman who reads it a personal kindness.'

Dickens opened the cover, pressing down on the spine to flatten the book. He picked up his pen and, choosing the first blank page he found, thought for a few moments before beginning to write:

To my friend, Robert Duckworth, and his son, of Manchester; a Christmas Present for showing me a Christmas Past and a Christmas yet to come.

The words brought back memories of a long walk through the streets of Manchester in early October, with Robert and Lizzie Burns showing him extraordinary sights he would not have seen otherwise.

He signed his name with a flourish and the whirlwind of curlicues that had become his trademark.

He rang the bell for his servant and whilst waiting for the man to arrive, dusted the wet ink with pounce, blowing on it to encourage drying.

The door opened and Topping stood in the doorway, a fleck of steamed pudding on the edge of his lip. Dickens had obviously disturbed the man's lunch.

He found a stout envelope and wrote the address on the cover, attaching a small note by way of explanation.

Dear Mrs Gaskell,

I have taken the liberty of sending you my latest novella. It is intended as a Christmas present for the guide you recommended during my time in Manchester, Robert Duckworth.

I wonder if I could trouble you to give it to him before Christmas if at all possible. I visited his abode on Newberry Street but I am not sure of his precise address in Manchester.

Thank you in advance.

I remain your honourable and admiring servant,

Charles Dickens

He placed the note carefully in the book, sealing the envelope with his wax seal. 'Please send this to Manchester. When will it arrive?'

'If it is sent by crack coach, around nineteen hours, Mr Dickens. The mail by train is quicker at just over twelve hours, but more expensive.'

'Send it by train.'

'Yes, Mr Dickens.'

The servant withdrew, taking the envelope and its precious book with him.

Dickens sat for a moment, remembering the debt he owed Robert Duckworth. Without him, this book may not have been written.

Then, he sat upright and took up his pen once more to send out more Christmas gifts.

There was much to be done today; a day wasted on others is not wasted on one.

CHAPTER ONE

Monday, December 16, 2019
Didsbury, Manchester

Jayne Sinclair was running late.

The clock said 11.30 and she was due at her meeting in town at noon.

Damn. Damn. Damn.

As ever, she had become engrossed in her research, losing complete track of time.

She wanted to do something special for her stepmother, Vera, this Christmas. Rather than go to one of the department stores and buy some perfume, or something equally impersonal, Jayne decided a complete family tree with beautiful calligraphy created by her friend, Carol, would be the perfect present.

Ever since Jayne had managed to find Vera's long-lost brother in Australia, it was something she had planned to do, but work, life and the day-to-day pressures of running her own business had meant the gift had always been postponed.

But Christmas was the time to give something special, wasn't it? And she knew Vera would be thrilled with it, something she would treasure.

Of course, time and other clients had meant Jayne could only start that morning. She had risen fairly early at 7.30 a.m., when it was still dark outside and the wind was howling through the leafless trees.

Mr Smith was already back from his nighttime activities in the suburbs of Manchester, hovering over his empty bowl. She fed and watered him as she fixed herself a coffee from her Nespresso machine.

The aroma of coffee filled the air as Jayne switched on her computer and logged on. From a file in the drawer, she took out a blank family tree chart and from her bag she pulled out her Montblanc pen.

It was one of her eccentricities. When she was creating a family tree, she always wrote in the brightest vermilion ink on a hard copy, transferring the details on to the computer later. It was a little old-fashioned but it was her way of commemorating the lives of the people she listed. On this sheet of paper, they were going to be remembered once again.

The dead brought back to life.

'Time to begin,' she said out loud.

Luckily, she had already done some of the work on Vera's maternal line, the Duckworths, last year when she had investigated the 'vanished son', as her stepmother called him. But it wouldn't hurt to re-check her sources. In genealogy, you can never check enough.

She uncapped the pen and wrote in Vera's maiden name – Vera Atkins. She could add the married names later along with those of her children.

But first she'd have a chat with Robert, her stepfather. Her feeling was the chart should focus on Vera, not on her life as a married woman.

She drew in two other boxes. One for Vera's full brother, Charles, born in 1949. The other was for her half-brother, Harry. He had been born as the result of a wartime liaison between Vera's mother and a soldier killed during the D Day landings.

The mother had given him up to a children's home, always intending to find him again once her life was settled. Unfortunately, before she could arrange his return, he was sent to Australia as part of a postwar exodus of child migrants.

He had suffered greatly at the hands of the Christian Brothers at the school in Bindoon, but had finally built a successful life for himself in Perth.

Despite never meeting for sixty-seven years, they had become instant friends when Vera flew to Australia to meet him. Every Sunday morning since, without fail, they chatted to each other on the phone, making up for all the lost time.

On the next line, Jayne wrote in Vera's parents' names and details, checking her notes for the exact dates of birth and death.

| Norman Atkins | 10.01.21 - 07.05.94. |
| Freda Duckworth | 10.04.26 - 10.06.10 |

There was always something comforting about seeing the names on the family tree, the boxes beginning to be filled in with names and dates.

Outside, the weather was cold, the wind howling and beating against the kitchen windows.

Inside, Jayne was focused on the task in hand. It was time to re-check the details of Vera's grandparents. She had done this quickly before, but now was the time to go into more detail.

She decided to write in the maternal line first, the Duckworths, as she already had notes from her previous work.

She dug out the file and wrote in the names and birth dates of Vera's maternal grandparents.

| Francis Duckworth | 1903 - 1967 |

Dora Burns   1905 - 1983

They had married in 1926, with Dora giving birth to Freda in April of the same year.

Jayne then wrote in the Duckworth great-grandparents and all their children, whom she had found in the 1911 Census. They had been living in Oldham at the time and there was an older person with the same surname living with them. Unfortunately, his relation to the head of the household had been left blank.

Thomas Henry Duckworth	1879 -1924
Eliza Duckworth	1874 -1931
Margaret Duckworth	1899 -????
Samuel Duckworth	1901 -????
Francis Duckworth	1903 -1966
Hermione Duckworth	1905 -????
Charles Duckworth	1854 -????

Thomas Henry and Eliza were very consistent; a child every two years, she thought.

Jayne wrote a couple of notes to herself to follow up next time she researched.

What was Eliza Duckworth's maiden name? What happened to their children? Dates of death? Marriages? Children?

Check out Charles Duckworth. Great-great-grandfather??? Great-great grand-uncle??

There were probably a whole host of relatives that Vera knew nothing about. Later, when Jayne had taken the family back to the 1881 Census she would link up with the Lost Cousins website to discover the names of these people.

That was all the research she had done in 2017 regarding Vera's maternal line. Time to bring the paternal line to the same level.

But first she decided another coffee was needed. When she was researching a family line, she lived on coffee. It was her fuel, keeping her going when she reached the inevitable brick walls.

She stood up, stretched and put a capsule in the Nespresso machine. 'Jewels', the marketing people called these things. What a load of tripe.

What had happened to the simple cup of coffee?

When she was growing up it was just a teaspoon of granules in a cup and hot water dumped on top. Now it was single country beans, roasted over banana leaves and picked by vestal virgins. There was even one coffee that came from the excreta of a type of civet cat.

She glanced across at Mr Smith.

'There's no way I'm drinking anything that's been through your guts.'

He pretended to be asleep, but his ears twitched, always a giveaway that he'd heard her.

The machine finished whirring and pouring. She picked up her espresso cup and smelt the aroma, taking a small sip of the dark, bitter coffee. Instantly, she felt a nice hit of caffeine kick in the back of her brain.

She had to admit it was far better than any of the instant coffee she had ever tried. Perhaps there was something in this idea of progress after all.

'Right, back to work.'

It was time to tackle Vera's father's family and see what secrets came to light.

CHAPTER TWO

October 3, 1843
Devonshire Terrace, London

Charles Dickens was late, but he comforted himself that he wasn't the late Charles Dickens.

He stepped out of Devonshire Terrace, making a mental note to remember the word 'play' for use in one of his serials.

The Hackney carriage was waiting outside his door, held open for him by his flame-haired servant, William Topping. Neither his wife nor his children had come to see him off, but he preferred it that way. Long emotional goodbyes were tedious, the stuff of novels rather than real life.

He heaved his carpetbag into the carriage. The inside stank of tobacco, a harsh pungent smell from a cheroot rather than the warm hug of a pipe. 'To Euston Station, cabbie. I would be much obliged if you could drive quickly, I'm late.'

The side of the cabbie's head appeared through the little window cut into the fabric of the roof. He touched the peak of his battered hat and said, 'As your honour pleases, a fast drive it is.'

The cabbie clicked his tongue three times and the carriage jerked forward, pulling out into the traffic, the clip clop of the horse's shoes resounding on the road.

'Won't be long, sir. Just up here on to the new road, past the university and we're there. Won't be more than two shakes of a donkey's leg.'

Dickens relaxed back into the horsehair seats, ignoring the smell. 'Thank you, cabbie.'

'It's Fezziwig, sir. Albert Fezziwig, late of the Second Dragoons, Lieutenant-Colonel Hamilton commanding and Waterloo, sir.'

'You were in the Scot's Greys?'

'Indeed I was, sir.' A face appeared in the window, a rugged scar running down across the left eye and on to the cheek. 'A French sword gave me this, sir, but he didn't give it no one else. I runs him through quicker than you can say "the Prince of Wales".'

'Do you remember the battle?'

'Not much, sir, to be honest. After I gets my wound, it's all a bit of a muddle. Luckily, I was saved by the surgeon, Mr Bell. Right good he was with a needle and cat gut.'

'You're lucky to be alive.'

'I counts my lucky stars every day, sir.' There was a long pause. 'You taking one of those new trains today, sir?'

'I am indeed.'

A long exhale of breath. 'You wouldn't catch me dead on one of those. Well, it ain't natural, is it? Going so fast pulled along by a monster.'

'It's a steam engine and the best ones can go at thirty miles an hour.'

'Oi, you, watch where you're going with that hoss!' A loud shout followed by a louder hawk and the sound of a gob of spit being expelled along with a wad of chewing tobacco. 'Goin' that fast is enough to make your head fall off. I thinks if God wanted us to go faster he would have made hosses with six legs.'

'Fezziwig, that's an interesting name.'

'Got it from my father, but don't know where he got it from, sir.'

The cab swung a hard left, throwing Dickens against the side.

'We's here now, sir, let me take you to the landing stage.'

The cabbie raced through the Doric portico, joining a long queue of Hackneys waiting to disgorge their passengers at the alighting point. Dickens leant forward to rap on the roof. 'Here will do, Mr Fezziwig.'

'That'll be two shillings, your honour. Plus an extra shilling for the speed on accounts of the hoss will need more oats this evening.' A hand came in through the hole, palm upwards. Dickens could see the dirt engrained into the creases of the palms.

'Here's five shillings, keep the change.'

The hand received the money and in the blink of an eye the door of the cab opened, Mr Fezziwig standing there, a broad smile across his face. 'It's been a pleasure to drive your honour. Will I be calling a porter? But I would h-advise they are thievin' bastards, beggin' your honour's pardon.'

'No, I won't be needing one, thank you.'

'No, thank you, your honour, for gracin' my 'umble cab. It ain't often I 'ave a famous writer in my cab. One day, I had that Mr Thackeray, but he ain't 'alf as good as you.'

'You've read my work?'

Mr Fezziwig laughed. 'By my word, you are a card, sir. Me reading? Not a chance. I fink the hoss could do a better job of reading than me.' The cabbie reached in and placed Dickens' bag in his hand. "Ave a good journey, sir.' He looked back as a puff of steam erupted from a platform. 'But rather you than me.'

Dickens walked away past the bowing Fezziwig. The concourse of the station was bustling with passengers, porters, and the myriad visitors who had come to see one of the wonders of the modern age; the steam engines being turned on their turntables to make their return journeys to Birmingham. On the left, a long queue snaked out in front of the booking office. Luckily, he had sent Topping down yesterday to buy the ticket.

Dickens spotted one of the station managers for the London and Birmingham Railway. 'The mail train for Birmingham?' he asked.

'Just in time, sir.' The man took out a silver hunter pocket watch. 'It departs on the dot at 9.45. Can't keep the Queen's mail waiting.'

'Yes, but which line is it?'

'The last one, sir. The engine is driven by my brother, James Duncan.'

'Here's my ticket.'

The station master took it and immediately his eyes lit up. 'The mail coach. Certainly, sir, shall I escort you, sir?'

'If you would be so kind, Mr Duncan.'

The man took Dickens' bag and hurried off to the far side of the station, weaving through the assembled people.

Despite having travelled by train many times before, Dickens never ceased to be amazed by the wonders of train travel.

The glass roof with its soaring iron pillars arced above his head. In front of him the engine steamed, sending clouds of white smoke into the air. Around the iron monster, engineers bustled, adding those finishing touches with oil cans that made them look busy. Dickens didn't know what they were doing, but he was content their tasks were necessary to help him arrive at his destination safely and securely.

They both hurried past the Post Office coach. Inside, Dickens could see a row of clerks sorting the mail.

The man stopped and pointed to the entrance of a carriage. 'Or would sir prefer to ride in the open in the cabriolet? The views can be stunning.'

'The carriage will be fine.'

'There are just four other passengers in the mail coaches today, sir. But the rest of the train is full. Will you be completing your journey in Birmingham?'

'No, I'm going on to Manchester.'

He opened the door. 'Certainly, sir. A station master will be waiting to escort you to the Manchester train at Curzon Street.'

'How long is the journey today?'

'Oh, very quick, sir, with James driving. Just five hours and ten minutes to Birmingham and another four hours to Manchester. With the transfer, you will be arriving in Manchester at 7.10 p.m. on the dot this evening.'

A loud toot from the engine, followed by a long hiss of steam.

'Please step aboard, sir, we are ready to depart. The steward will take your bag.'

A white gloved hand reached down. Dickens' bag disappeared into the coach.

'Thank you, Mr Duncan.'

'No, thank you, Mr Dickens. It will be a pleasure to have a famous author on our train today.'

For the second time that morning, Dickens was reminded what a pleasure it was to have him enjoy the transport.

He only wished there were more pleasures in his life. The recent news about Chuzzlewit had definitely destroyed his mood.

He climbed aboard the carriage. Perhaps the journey could help him forget his troubles. He certainly hoped so.

For the first time since the publication of Sketches, his future as an author didn't look so rosy. Had he become like Icarus, flying too close to the sun?

CHAPTER THREE

Monday, December 16, 2019
Didsbury, Manchester

Jayne took her seat back in front of the computer. Now it was time to tackle the paternal line; the Atkins.

She logged on to the FreeBMD site to search the Births, Marriages and Deaths indexes and typed 'Norman Atkins' into the fields, adding the date – 1921 – and the district where he was born, Oldham.

Just one result popped up on her screen almost immediately.

Atkins, Norman T.
Mother's maiden name: Radcliffe.
Registration district: Oldham

It was catalogued under January to March with a number of 9c, 1441.

'We've got a start.'

This time, the cat looked up at her for a second before returning to the far more important task of cleaning his paws.

Jayne went to Ancestry.com and in the search box typed the name and birth date again, requesting only results from England as she knew exactly where he was born and he had never lived overseas.

'With a bit of luck, there might even be an existing family tree. What do you say to that, Mr Smith?'

The cat said nothing, turning his back on her completely.

Since her separation from her husband, Jayne worried that she might become a cat lady, one of those women who talk to their cats just to hear the sound of a human voice. In the middle ages, she might even have been tried as a witch, with Mr Smith hung, drawn and quartered as her familiar.

She'd had relationships, of course. The most recent, with a lecturer from Manchester University called Tom Carpenter, had fizzled out of its own accord. The spark just wasn't there. They remained friends but it was obvious it wasn't going to develop into anything deeper. Jayne could see little point in being with somebody just because they were a warm body or because she was lonely.

The way she saw it, if there was no passion, there was no life. At the moment, her passion was her work and her family. Nothing else mattered. When she met the right person she would know, but that was yet to happen.

She returned to the screen. Unhappily, nobody else was researching Norman Atkins' family. Despite there being over 1000 hits, only two were applicable for the search.

The first was a transcript of his death certificate in 1994, which confirmed the dates of his birth and death but gave very little other information.

The second was much better. It was the 1939 England and Wales Register, taken just after the outbreak of the Second World War. Jayne was surprised to see Norman Atkins' name there, as his birth was less than 100 years ago. Had someone informed the Census of his death?

The details were wonderful.

286 Oldham Road				
Atkins, George	M	17 Sept 92	Married	Driver. AR Warden
Atkins, Mildred	F	20 July 96	Married	House-wife

| Atkins, Norman | M | 10 Jan 21 | Single | Cotton Piecer |

Jayne punched the air, thanking the gods of genealogy. She now had Vera's paternal grandparents. She typed George's name into the Findmypast website. This was another of her eccentricities, using more than one family history search engine. Sometime, the results were slightly different depending on the documents the site held.

She quickly scanned the leading results. There did seem to be a listing in the 1911 Census. But one result caught her eye. It was from the *Manchester Evening News*, dated December 27,1944.

BOMB DROPPED ON OLDHAM ROAD, 7 DEAD

Christmas Eve was a dark day in Oldham which will never be forgotten as long as men or women reside in the town.

A flying bomb dropped on Oldham Road at 5.30 p.m. on Christmas Eve. Residents of numbers 286 and 288 were just sitting down to their evening tea when the bomb landed, killing everybody in both houses.

The devastating blast from the flying bomb took the lives of two family members residing in number 286, and a husband, wife and three children resident in number 288.

Nobody else was injured.

The names of the dead have been released. They are:

George Atkins, aged 52
Mildred Atkins, aged 48
Thomas Lord, aged 34
Elspeth Lord, aged 32
Michael Lord, aged 6
Peter Lord, aged 4
Catherine Lord, aged 2

The relatives of the deceased have been informed; they include two members of the armed forces serving overseas.

It is believed the original target of the raid was Manchester but that the doodlebug had fallen short after running out of fuel.

Dorothy Settle, aged 10, told the *Evening News*:

"I was passing by, walking home from the shops, when there was a drone overhead. Suddenly the sound stopped and ten seconds later there was a terrible blast. I don't know what happened after that as I went unconscious but they said I had to be pulled out of the wreckage."

It was a lucky escape for young Dorothy.

The public must remember to be extra vigilant over these holidays. The Ministry of Information reminds people that the Nazis are targeting England with their new V-1 bombs. If you hear one overhead, do not look at it but take cover immediately until it has passed.

An immense wave of sadness passed over Jayne. This must have been one of the last V-1 attacks of the war. What a senseless waste of young lives. And at Christmas. A horrible time to be told of the deaths of your mother and father.

What about Norman? Was he serving in the Army at this time? Poor man.

Jayne printed out the article. It would go in Vera's file, along with the family tree.

She glanced out of the patio window. She had been so engrossed in her work, the sun had already risen without her realising it. There was little difference in the light, however; the sky had that dull grey dishcloth colour, as if a vast reservoir of dirty water was waiting to be dumped on to the waiting citizens of Manchester.

Jayne stretched, elongating her body and groaning. Being hunched over a computer day in, day out was not the best training for the body. She must rearrange her pilates classes, anything to release the tension in her shoulders and back.

She glanced out of the patio window again. It wasn't raining yet but it was certainly thinking long and hard about it.

She mustn't forget her umbrella and her heavy coat when she went out. Manchester in the middle of December was not the most comfortable place to be if you didn't wrap up well.

Jayne returned to her screen. Time to check up on the 1911 Census return for George Atkins.

She brought up Ancestry.com again and typed George Atkins into the search function. By her reckoning, he would have been nineteen at the time of the Census.

No results for a George Atkins in Oldham. She broadened the search to include the rest of Lancashire. One result came up, written in the handwriting of the man who was Vera's great-grandfather.

Name	Age	Status	Work	Birth
John Atkins	44	Married	Scrounger	Manc
Ethel Atkins	42	Married	House-wife	Man
William Atkins	21	Single	Scrounger	Manc
George Atkins	19	Single	Coal Carter	Manc

But was this the right George Atkins?

Ancestry.com offered a few suggestions to follow up. One was a notice of banns in Manchester for a wedding to a Mildred Goodall in 1913. The Christian name of George's wife certainly checked out, but the change of location from Oldham to Manchester was a concern.

Jayne pencilled the names into the Family Tree and added a note to herself to ask Vera discreetly about her great-grandfather.

She noticed the listed profession of George's father: "scrounger". He must have been a rag-and-bone man. A sort of *Steptoe and Son*, going round collecting and recycling people's junk. George himself was a coal-man, driving a horse and cart, delivering the coal that heated most houses in those days. It was not such a great leap to imagine changing that profession to being a driver. It was simply a matter of exchanging a horse and cart for a petrol engine.

There were two other pieces of information suggested by Ancestry.com, both military records for the First World War. An attestation record and a pension record. Jayne clicked the first link.

Despite being married in 1913, George joined up just over three weeks after the declaration of war with Germany. He must have been one of those young men driven by patriotic fervour to accept the King's Shilling in the early days of the war.

Jayne made a note of the information listed on the attestation papers.

Name: **George Atkins**
Where Born: **Ardwick, Manchester**
Age: **22 years 8 months**
Trade: **Driver**

The profession certainly indicated that this was the right man. She also noticed he had already upgraded himself from a coal carter to a driver, a much more skilled trade.

She carried on reading the document.

Resided in your father's house for three years? Yes
Are you an Apprentice? No
Are you married? Yes
Have you ever been imprisoned? No
Have you ever been in the Services? No
Are you willing to be enlisted? Yes

The document was signed by George Atkins and the recruiting officer, Sergeant Osborne, and dated August 30, 1914.

Jayne went back to the top of the document to make a note of his service number to check out his medal awards later. Strange – he had three numbers, two of which were crossed out.

~~19683~~
~~11746~~
38675

The answer lay on the other side of the document. George Atkins had served in three different regiments, receiving a new number each time.

King's Own Scottish Borderers
Border Regiment
Machine Gun Corps

Jayne knew the first two well. Perhaps George was transferred out of a Scottish Border Regiment to an English Border Regiment because he couldn't understand the accents. Unless there was a complete file for George, they would never know. The absence of a link on Ancestry.com to a record suggested his file was one of the many that had been destroyed by fire in World War Two. Somehow the attestation and pension records had survived.

The third unit mentioned was interesting. Jayne checked out the Machine Gun Corps on Wikipedia. It wasn't founded until October 1915, when the top brass had finally realised that machine guns were important to trench warfare. There was a surprising line in the article, though. '*It had a less enviable record for its casualty rate. Some 170,500 officers and men served in the MGC, with 62,049 becoming casualties, including 12,498 killed, earning it the nickname "the Suicide Club".*'

George had served in the 'suicide club'. What a horrible name for a military unit. But behind the name was a dark, self-deprecating sense of humour that was typically British, even in times of war.

A shudder went down her back as she thought of the horror of the name.

She was tempted to do even more research on the Machine Gun Battalions, but realised that she could vanish into a black hole of documents, never to appear again.

'Stay focused, Jayne.'

She clicked on the pension record dated 1919, it's title announcing the subject matter in solid black capitals.

FIRST AWARD – SOLDIER

Name:	George Atkins
Regiment:	Machine Gun Corps, 11th Batt.
Date of Discharge:	12.4.19
Regimental No.:	38675
Address:	29 Mount St., Ardwick.

Jayne quickly checked back to the address on the 1911 Census.

29, Mount St., Ardwick.

It matched.

Jayne punched the air again, causing Mr Smith to open one eye cautiously before closing it slowly, adjusting his position slightly to become more comfortable and going back to sleep.

The address was exactly the same. George and his wife must have continued to live with his father after they were married. It was the man she was looking for.

She checked out the rest of the document displayed on her screen.

Rank for Pension:	Private
Age:	28
Nature of Disability:	Code no. 43
Disability:	Debility
Degree of Disablement:	30%
Weekly Rate:	12s 0d
Allowance for Wife:	5s 3d

It was unsigned, but dated February 14, 1920.

Valentine's Day.

George received a love letter from the Ministry of Pensions nine months after his discharge, awarding him a pension for 'debility'.

What was that?

Jayne went back online to try to understand what it meant. She quickly found out that the large numbers of people being injured in World War One led to the standardisation of pension awards.

The loss of two or more limbs, for example, entitled a man to a 100% pension, whereas amputation of a leg above the knee was assessed at 60% and below the knee at 50%.

Psychological and functional somatic disorders, such as shell-shock, were more difficult to diagnose but were for the first time beginning to be accepted as illnesses. In the years after 1918, a total of 817 soldiers were diagnosed with Neurasthenia and 568 with Debility.

Jayne recognised these diagnoses. George was suffering from what today we would call PTSD, or Post-Traumatic Stress Disorder. Not surprising as he was a part of an elite unit called the 'Suicide Club'.

She quickly made notes. None of this information was strictly part of the Tree she was creating for Vera, but it was part of the narrative of the family. Jayne believed strongly that family history was made up of people's stories. Sometimes you could recreate these stories from documents. It was all part of understanding where one came from and what motivated our ancestors.

She glanced up and saw the clock.

'Damn. Damn. Damn.'

11.30. Where had the time gone?

As usual she had been so lost in her research that she had lost track of time and was now half an hour behind schedule. Her meeting was in the centre of Manchester and, depending on the traffic and finding somewhere to park, the journey could take twenty minutes or an hour.

Luckily, she knew the centre of the city well; she'd spent two years there as a young copper based in the town hall nick. She wondered if Sergeant McNally was still on the front desk. A grumpy old bugger who'd seen it all but had taught her everything she knew about reading people.

'Look at their posture. The ones who are ready to fight are tense, their hands often clenching and unclenching. You then decide it's time to defuse the situation, make a joke or try to understand what's happening. It's not the violent ones I worry about, though. It's the ones who won't look you in the eye, the ones who keep their head down all the time and mumble an answer. Soften your voice and try to engage with them. If they don't respond, put them on watch, got it?'

'I think so, Sarge.'

'It's Sergeant or Ed, Jayne. I can't stand Sarge.'

'Right, Sarge. I mean, Sergeant.'

She was a young naïve copper then, just starting out. But under McNally's tutorship she learnt more in six months pounding the beat in Manchester than she had in six years at school. Should she go back after the meeting and see if any of the old gang were still there? Or should she drive out to see Robert and Vera? She hadn't seen her stepfather for three days and it would be great to go to see him.

Perhaps. She'd see how the client meeting went first.

She glanced at the clock again.

Damn. Damn. Damn.

She rushed upstairs and quickly changed into a shirt and slacks, tying her long hair into a tight ponytail.

In the hallway, she grabbed her jacket and Marmot padded coat. Not the most elegant of clothes, as it made her look like a pregnant penguin, but it kept her warm and dry even in the heaviest of Manchester downpours.

She popped her head into the kitchen to check Mr Smith had water, then rushed out of the door. She could put a dab of lipstick on in the car at the traffic lights if she needed it.

Putting the BMW into gear, she headed out past Parrs Wood, turning left on to the A34. If there weren't too many red lights, it would be a straight run past Manchester Grammar and on to the A6 into the town centre.

She put an old Bowie CD into the player and chose 'Jean Genie' to put her in the mood. As the first chords belted out, she thought about the person she was meeting, Michael Underwood.

The call had come in yesterday. 'Hello, is that Jayne Sinclair, the genealogist?'

'Speaking.'

'My name is Underwood. I saw your website and it says that you specialise in genealogical investigations, is that correct?' The voice was educated and urbane, with no hint of a Manchester accent.

'I specialise in difficult investigations, particularly ones where there may be a brick wall that seems insurmountable. I usual find if you work hard and dig deep, an answer can be discovered. But there are no guarantees. Sometimes the documentation just isn't there, particularly far back in the past.'

'I understand. Could we meet up? I think I may have a job for you.'

Jayne sucked in air between her teeth. 'I'm not sure I can take any new work on at the moment, Mr Underwood. I'm very busy and it is extremely close to the Christmas holiday.'

The truth was she didn't have too much on, but she wanted to treat herself to a break over the festive period. Last year, she had worked right up until Christmas Day on the Roberts case. It had been wonderful finally finding the truth about the Christmas Truce, but it had been exhausting.

This year, she was determined to take life a bit easier until the New Year. She felt quite tired at the moment and a little unsettled.

'Let's meet up, at least. I think I have a very interesting case that may challenge your skills.'

'I don't know...'

'Please. It's important to myself and my colleague and we don't have much time. Let me explain to you in person. I'll even buy the coffee and cake. Please…'

There was a pleading in the voice. For some reason, Jayne found herself saying yes.

Now here she was, parking in Addington Street and rushing to the meeting in the Mackie Mayor, a café-cum-restaurant in the old Smithfield market.

One thing had intrigued her about the call.

Why was this job so important to this man?

CHAPTER FOUR

October 3, 1843
The train from London to Birmingham

Dickens relaxed back in his seat, and stared out of the window as the train gave a final toot and pulled out of the station. Luckily, he had this carriage to himself and, as there were only three other passengers, two of whom seemed to be elderly spinsters from Eastbourne, he was unlikely to be disturbed.

The train gathered speed as it crossed over Hampstead Road. On the right, the slums of Camden were smothered in a brown fog. Not a place of happy memories for Dickens; he had lived in Bayham Street, in a small tenement with a wretched little back garden abutting a squalid court. It had been the start of the bad times for his family. His father was constantly in debt, living from day to day. Debts which would take him and the family off to Marshalsea to reside at his creditor's pleasure. While Dickens himself was abandoned and forced to work in a blacking factory off the Strand.

He smiled ruefully at the memory. Sitting in a window facing on to the street, affixing the labels by hand on to the blacking bottles while passers-by craned in to watch his work. A horrible, wretched time, slaving twelve hours a day for Mr Warren and barely getting enough to eat, living on bowls of gruel and scraps of leftovers.

Abandoned at twelve to live by his wits.

A shiver went down his spine.

Never again would he face those times. He would rather write his fingers to the bone than ever suffer those feelings of loneliness and fear and hunger.

But it might come to that if he were not careful. He'd received news from his bankers, Coutts, that morning. He was overdrawn, disastrously so. Sales of *Chuzzlewit* were not going well, the story did not seem to have resonated with readers in the way his previous serialisations had done. He had spent many worrying hours trying to work out why and what he should do about it

Added to these pressures, Catherine was pregnant. He only had to look at her these days and she would find herself with child. And to tap it all, to add the final shoe to the horse of penury, his father had visited him two weeks ago, explaining that he was in debt again. 'A trifling sum' he'd said – they were always 'trifling sums– ' as he asked for another bail-out. Just a few days ago, Dickens had received a threatening letter from his father demanding the money immediately. Money he didn't have any more.

As ever, he was amazed and confounded by the audacity and ingratitude of the man. A man who had put his own son to work in a blacking factory rather than send him to school.

He ran his fingers through his long dark hair. Didn't he realise the life of an author was one of constant fear of running out of ideas, being discovered as a talentless hack or having the public turn from fawning over him to sinking their teeth into his body?

What if his success so far had been a flash in the pan? Perhaps he would soon be discovered by the public as the charlatan author he was, not fit to put pen to paper.

Look what had happened to his friend, Harrison Ainsworth. His readers turned from devoted subjects to merciless assassins of his reputation because of the dubious testimony of a dubious servant who had killed his master.

Even his damned publishers seemed to be losing confidence in him. The venerable firm of Chapman & Hall were invoking some obscure clause in his contract to ensure he paid them for the pleasure of publishing his books.

Again, with money he didn't have and couldn't spare.

Cant, humbug and arrant hypocrisy. His solicitor had advised him the contracts were unfair, but in his desire to see *Boz* published, he had signed them anyway.

Outside, the trees and hedgerows were displaying the colours of autumn in a rainbow of browns, greens, yellows, golds and reds. The smoke, dust and dirt of London had been left far behind.

He loved this time of year in the English countryside, when the air had a freshness, a clarity far removed from the brown fogs and clamour of the city.

In a field bordering the railway line, a horse kicked up its rear legs and raced away from the noise of the train, its mane flowing in the wind and its head held high, glorying in the power of its muscles.

He made a mental note of the image for use in his books. He recognised his style; he was like a magpie picking up ideas, images, words and speech from everywhere, and filtering them to create his novels.

The train pilled away from the horse despite its speed and power.

'If only I could be so free,' Dickens whispered to nobody but himself. Then, 'Enough!' he said, louder, causing the steward to come forward to the compartment to ask if he required anything.

Dickens shook his head.

'Some tea, sir?'

'No, thank you,' he insisted.

The steward nodded his head and withdrew.

Dickens pulled out the recent parliamentary report on *Child Labourers in Britain's Factories,* written by Thomas Southwood Smith, and began reading it all over again.

It was shocking. He had promised to write a pamphlet in support of this cause but he wanted to see for himself the conditions under which the children worked before he did so.

But what good would another pamphlet do? There were thousands of such political broadsheets on the streets, and in the libraries and bookshops of London.

There must be something more he could do, but he didn't know what.

He had recently visited one of the Ragged Schools, created to educate the children of the poor. The visit had been depressing; there were so many children out there in dire straits; with little or no food to eat and even less to feed their minds.

What could he do to highlight the problem? To force people to take some sort of action, however small?

Today's journey to Manchester was a beginning.

Along with Disraeli and Cobden, he had been asked to give a speech in support of a fund-raising soiree at the Athenaeum in Manchester, a library and meeting place for the education of the middle and working classes.

It was a start, a small start in the process of universal education which he felt was key to the problems of the country. If everybody could read and write, surely they would make better choices about their lives and their futures.

It was a hope, a small hope.
He checked his speech once again.

Dear Friends and Colleagues,

It gives me great pleasure to give a speech in support of this temple to learning; the Athenaeum. Here, it is hoped the residents of Manchester will discover the glories, knowledge, power and beauty of learning, books and reading.

They may even discover my own worthless attempts at literature…

He stopped. It was hopeless. The tone was wrong. Too self-satisfied, too self-congratulatory, as if by merely funding a library they had achieved their goal of improving society.

He threw it down on the seat in front of him.

It was one of those days; the best of times and the worst of times.

He prayed it would get better.

CHAPTER FIVE

Monday, December 16, 2019
Mackie Mayor, Old Smithfield Market, Manchester

Jayne hurried along the street towards the Mackie Mayor.

This area was once the centre of what was one of the commercial hubs of Manchester. After a long period of decline, it had been rebranded as the Northern Quarter, with old mills, warehouses and factories transformed into apartments for bearded millennials and their partners.

Distressed was the designer style, and it always distressed Jayne when she had to visit the area, with its myriad cafés furnished with second-hand chairs and tables from Oxfam.

As she entered the old Smithfield Market, now completely repurposed as a café-cum-eating-hall, she was already beginning to regret agreeing to the meeting so close to Christmas.

Near the entrance, an elegantly dressed man stood up from a long communal table. 'Jayne Sinclair, I presume? I recognise you from the picture on your website.'

'Mr Underwood?'

'The one and only. But please call me Michael. Take a seat. What would you like? Are you hungry? They do a lovely bowl of ramen. Or a slice of pizza?'

'I'm not hungry, thanks. But a latte would be great.'

'One latte, coming up.'

He went off to the counter to order, without introducing her to the man sitting next to him.

For a moment, both regarded each other awkwardly before Jayne stuck out her hand and said, 'Jayne Sinclair. Are you with Mr Underwood?'

The man rose and touched the fingertips of her hand before sitting back down quickly. 'Sorry, I'm not good in social situations,' he said, without looking at her.

Jayne looked around her. Most of the tables were full of young people talking earnestly. With the large double-height ceiling, the level of noise was almost deafening. A soundtrack of Christmas songs playing in the background only added to the sound levels.

'Don't worry, neither am I,' she said before pointing to the bench. 'Do you mind if I sit down here opposite you?'

For the first time he looked at her, smiled and nodded his head.

Michael Underwood returned as she sat down. 'They will deliver the coffee shortly. I see you've met Ronald.' Underwood reached over and patted the man's shoulder as he sat down. 'Don't worry, he's a bit shy.'

Jayne knew that it was more than shyness. The man was definitely uncomfortable being surrounded by so many people. 'We can go somewhere with less people if you want, Ronald?'

The man shook his head without looking at her. 'No, we're here now, might as well stay.'

Michael Underwood rubbed his hands together. 'Good, that's decided.' The skin of his face had a slight glossy tinge to it and he was wearing a very expensive-smelling aftershave. Too much of it, unfortunately.

'You may be wondering why I asked you to come here today.'

'It had crossed my mind.'

Michael Underwood waved his arms expansively. 'Look around you, what do you see?'

Jayne followed his arms. Mackie Mayor occupied a beautiful old market building with light streaming in through the glass skylights, and thin, cast-iron columns soaring up to the double-storey roof, finished at the top with elegantly moulded finials. A modern staircase led to a mezzanine floor with distressed whitewashed walls. Here and there, a few desultory attempts had been made to give the place a Christmas spirit; red and silver tinsel, a plastic tree surrounded by fake presents and plastic candy canes.

The various food vendors were arrayed around the sides of the hall, displaying their specialities on chalk boards; wines, coffee, tacos, pizza, ramen, brunch, sandwiches, pad thai, fried chicken. All the modern food groups from all over the world. She had been to a similar repurposed marketplace in Altrincham. Here the crowd was younger, more egalitarian.

'It's a lovely space,' she finally said, noncommittally.

'It is, isn't it? It's the former Smithfield meat market, built and opened by the Manchester Corporation way back in 1858. A wonderful example of the sort of elegant but functional buildings created during that period. Manchester was at the height of its importance; the Art Exhibition opened by Queen Victoria had been held at Old Trafford, the city was the world's centre for cotton manufacturing, the mills were running round the clock and the city was booming. This market is almost an exemplar of the city itself. It gradually grew less and less important, finally becoming derelict in 1972 and remaining unused and almost forgotten until recently, when this place was created.'

He glanced around the open space. 'It has that semi-industrial feel of SoHo in New York, doesn't it?'

Jayne had never been to New York – it was on her bucket list – but she could imagine a place like this in the city. Ronald shifted uneasily in his seat, looking across at her through his fringe.

'Thanks for the history lesson, Mr Underwood, but what has this to do with our meeting?'

'It's Michael, and I assure you it has a lot to do with our meeting, Jayne. I thought we should get together here because it imbues the essence of the case I would like you to investigate.'

She was intrigued. 'Please explain.'

'I will, but let me first tell you who I am and where Ronald fits in with all this.'

Ronald was staring at her again. Jayne was tempted to ask his surname but didn't want to put him under any pressure as he was already looking so uncomfortable. Was the man autistic or did he have Aspergers?

'As I said, my name is Michael Underwood. I run an auction house, you may have heard of it? Underwood and Little?'

Jayne shook her head.

The man seemed slightly miffed. 'No matter. We specialise in finding unusual objects and marketing them to a select clientele.'

'So you don't have a gavel and desk then?'

Underwood laughed. 'Occasionally, but I don't use my gavel that much any more these days. It is much easier to market our items to a few select customers and then hold an auction online.'

'Go on...'

He pointed to the man sitting next to him. 'Ronald Welsh is one of my searchers.'

'Searcher?'

'I discover unusual and valuable things. I'm very good at it.'

Underwood interrupted quickly. 'Ronald is one of our best searchers.'

'The best. I'm the best.'

'Ronald is one of our best searchers,' emphasised Underwood. 'Recently he discovered a very valuable item that we are going to market to our customers.'

'I found it in a charity shop in Shudehill. Got it for one pound fifty pence. Knew it was valuable as soon as I saw it.'

'This is all very interesting, but where do I come in?' asked Jayne.

Underwood reached down inside a brown leather attaché case that was on the seat beside him. He pulled out a sealed plastic wallet. Inside was a small, pinkish book. 'This is what we want you to investigate.'

Jayne laughed. 'I'm a genealogist not a book collector, Mr Underwood. I think you have the wrong person.'

Underwood carefully put on a pair of cotton gloves, before opening the plastic file and bringing out the book. Holding it carefully, he presented the cover to Jayne. She reached out to hold it and he jerked backwards

'No offence, Jayne, but we don't allow anybody to touch the book. The acids in the sweat on the ends of your fingers could damage it.'

She stared at the title, embossed in gold letters on the cover:

A Christmas Carol

'What you see in front of you is a first edition of Dickens' famous Christmas novella. It was first published on December 19, 1843 for the exorbitant price of five shillings. This copy, being in such fine condition, is now worth something in the region of thirty thousand pounds.'

Jayne exhaled loudly. 'I had no idea a book could be so valuable. But I'm still trying to understand how I fit into all of this.'

'It's quite simple, Jayne. With your help we could double or even triple this price.'

Ronald smiled and nodded excitedly.

Jayne nodded. 'Now you have me interested.'

CHAPTER SIX

Monday, December 16, 2019
Mackie Mayor, Old Smithfield Market, Manchester

'You say you found this in a charity shop?'

'I discovered it hidden at the bottom of a box of books donated by a well-wisher.'

'Shouldn't it belong to the charity then?'

Ronald looked sheepish.

Underwood interrupted. 'We paid the asking price for it from the shop. The manager priced it and I went in to buy it myself. All is above board.'

'Is it? Shouldn't you have told the charity shop about the book?'

Ronald again looked sheepish.

'Everything is above board, Jayne. It's no different from finding a valuable antique at a car boot sale and discovering the real value on *Antiques Roadshow*. The only difference is Ronald spotted it first before anybody else.'

'How do you know it isn't a fake?'

Ronald suddenly became animated again. 'Please, Mrs Sinclair.' He gestured at the book. 'It's a first edition, first issue, the very rare and so-called "trial issue", with the title page printed in red and green and the half-title printed in green.'

He paused for a second to take a breath. 'The front cover and spine are decoratively stamped and lettered in gilt, and all the edges are gilt too. The binding matches Todd's first impression, first issue, with a close space between the blind-stamped border and gilt wreath equal to fourteen millimetres. More importantly, for the cover, the "D" in "Dickens" is in perfect, unbroken condition.'

He gestured to Underwood, who opened the book to the title page.

'See, the title is printed in green and red. Dickens was closely involved in the printing of this first edition. He even paid for it himself when the publishers refused.'

Jayne leant in closer to read the text.

'A Christmas Carol' was in bright red. Beneath it, the words 'In Prose' were in a darker green, followed by 'Being A Ghost Story of Christmas', which was also in green an on separate lines. The author's name came next, in bigger type and in bright red: Charles Dickens.

'At the bottom, the title page continues with the words "original illustrations by John Leech" and the publishers, "Chapman & Hall", and ends with the date MDCCCLXIII.' Ronald waved his hand and Underwood turned the page.

The name of the book was repeated, and on the next page, an exquisite illustration of a plump couple dancing under a sprig of mistletoe.

Jayne frowned. She had read *A Christmas Carol* when she was young and had seen the numerous adaptations of it that seemed to be shown every Christmas. What was the name of the couple again?

As if reading her mind, Ronald answered. 'It's Mr and Mrs Fezziwig at their Christmas party.'

Jayne remembered the story now. It was a scene shown by the Ghost of Christmas Present to Ebenezer Scrooge. 'Couldn't somebody have simply copied this? Like *The Hitler Diaries* and other fakes?'

A long sigh from Ronald. 'The vertically ribbed cloth is in the original cinnamon, yellow coated endpapers, the size is small octavo and, most importantly, the first chapter is entitled "Stave 1". In later editions, the number "1" was written in letters as "one". Even better, two Americans, Calhoun and Heaney, recorded twenty-two inscribed examples of A Christmas Carol in their 1945 pamphlet, and this example was not among them.'

'Which makes it even more valuable,' interrupted Underwood.

'Why is it in such good condition?' Jayne asked.

'When I found it, the book was chemised in a red cloth slipcase. The spine of the slipcase has five raised bands and two green morocco labels lettered with the words "Volume One" in gilt but no indication of which book was inside. It's the reason it lay undiscovered for so long.' Ronald sat back. 'I know my job, Mrs Sinclair, and this is a Dickens first edition.'

'So it's real, not fake. You still haven't explained why you need my help?'

Underwood carefully turned the pages back to the beginning of the book. 'As you will see, Jayne, on the verso of the front endpaper is an inscription.'

Once more Jayne leant in to read the elegant script, written in fading black ink.

To my friend, Robert Duckworth, and his son, of Manchester; a Christmas Present for showing me a Christmas Past and a Christmas yet to come.

'Is that signed by who I think?' asked Jayne.
Both Michael Underwood and Ronald Welsh nodded.

The signature was strong and supple, ending with a tornado of curlicues that came to a point, suggesting the vast energy of the man.

'Charles Dickens?'

They both nodded again. 'Look at the date,' said the auctioneer.

Jayne peered down at the date next to the signature, written out in words without punctuation.

Nineteenth December 1843.

'It's the exact date when *A Christmas Carol* was first published.'

Jayne looked at the message again. 'The name, Robert Duckworth – it's also the surname of one of my stepmother's ancestors.'

The two men looked at each other. 'That's interesting. Do you think they could be related?'

And then a light bulb went off in Jayne's head. 'I see now what you want me to do. You want me to find out who Robert Duckworth was?'

Michael Underwood smiled broadly. 'Precisely, Jayne. But even more, we want you to find if he has any living descendants.'

CHAPTER SEVEN

Monday, December 16, 2019
Mackie Mayor, Old Smithfield Market, Manchester

Jayne checked the inscription again. 'This man, if he ever existed, could have lived anywhere in the UK. It would be like looking for a needle in a whole field of haystacks.'

Underwood smiled. 'We didn't say this was going to be easy, Jayne. If it was, we would do it ourselves.' He glanced across at Ronald as if weighing up whether to say more. 'The inscription says "of Manchester" and so we believe this man was living in the city at the time.'

'How do you know this?'

Ronald jumped in. 'We know Dickens travelled to Manchester in early October to deliver a speech at the inaugural soiree in support of the Athenaeum – the building is part of Manchester Art Gallery now. He also spent time with his sister, Frances, who was a music teacher and married to a man called Henry Burnett. They were living in Higher Ardwick.'

Jayne was writing all these details down in her notebook.

Ronald let her finish and then carried on speaking. 'In the Dickens family her usual nickname was Fan, or Fanny.'

Jayne dug out a half-remembered fact from her schooldays, hidden in the depths of her brain. 'Isn't Bob Cratchit's wife called Fan?'

'You remember the book well, Jayne,' said Michael Underwood.

'Even more, Frances and Henry Burnett had a severely disabled son, called Harry. He could have been the inspiration behind the character of Tiny Tim,' added Ronald.

Jayne stopped writing and looked up. 'Interesting.'

'And there are more links to Manchester. Dickens started writing *A Christmas Carol* sometime around October 15, 1843 – just ten days after he had visited Manchester. There are no clues in his letters to indicate where he got the inspiration for the book, but the visit to Manchester seems to have been followed by a furious bout of writing. He finished the novella in just six weeks, at the end of November.'

'But the novel is set in London.'

'True, but we believe the inspiration, and indeed some of the characters, may have been from Manchester,' said Underwood.

'There's even a clue in one of John Leech's illustrations.' Ronald nodded at Michael Underwood and the man turned over the pages of the book again. It was like a Morecambe and Wise double act without the jokes.

Underwood finally stopped at a black-and-white illustration entitled 'Ignorance and Want'.

'Dickens was intimately involved in the creation of the illustrations for the novel. If you look at the background for this one, what does it look like to you?'

Jayne stared at the picture. 'Mills and chimneys bellowing smoke.'

'Exactly. Not London at all, but Manchester.'

Jayne thought for a moment. Around her the bustle and noise of the market suddenly seemed louder, reflecting off the high ceiling and the cast-iron pillars. 'Let me get this right,' she finally said, prodding her notebook with her pencil. 'You are suggesting that the story of *A Christmas Carol* was inspired by Manchester, and particularly by the man to whom Dickens inscribed the dedication on the front leaf of this book?'

Underwood clapped his hands. 'Exactly, Jayne, you have it in one.'

'But why is this important?'

'In one word: provenance. That is, if we can prove the book was given to a man who inspired one of the major characters, then we can almost certainly triple the value. The Dickens fanatics in the States would clamour to get a copy. And if we can link it to a modern family in Manchester, well, it's a great human interest story for the tabloids.'

'And again, the price would go up?'

'Exactly,' both men said at the same time.

Jayne thought for a long time. The story intrigued her and, even more, the challenge brought out her competitive nature. Could she use her genealogical skills to find this man? But it was time to be realistic. 'You know, he may not have existed, and even if he did, the documentation for the period is sketchy at best.'

'We know it's a long shot, but it's worth a try, isn't it?'

'There must be a catch.'

The two men looked at each other.

'Well,' said Underwood, 'there is a small one. The online auction for the book has been set for December nineteenth.'

'The 176th anniversary of the book's publication,' said Ronald.

'But that's only three days away.'

'Exactly,' both men said again.

CHAPTER EIGHT

October 3, 1843
London Road Station, Manchester

For the last few minutes, the green of the countryside had gradually given way to the market gardens and then the beginning of housing and streets. Dickens relaxed, realising his journey was finally at an end.

He pulled out the gold hunter pocket watch from his emerald-green waistcoat and checked the time: 7.10 p.m. The train was right on time, as predicted by the station master nine hours ago. The speed of modern life never ceased to amaze Dickens, with past, present and future all melding together as if one. It was something he would have to consider for his next book. How man's relationship with time had changed from the carefree vagueness of youth to the specificity of the modern day.

As the train chugged along a curve and the sun's dying rays vanished beneath the horizon, the city of Manchester came into view as a dark dirty-grey cloud of smoke with tall chimneys hidden inside.

He wondered how his sister, Fanny, and her husband were surviving in this dark place. They were both music teachers, having met at the Royal College of Music.

Both had moved north only a year ago and Dickens missed his sister immensely. She was the rock of the family, the one he had always turned to in his youth when he wanted good advice or a friendly ear to listen to his many problems.

His mother, unfortunately, was not a sympathetic soul. She had encouraged him to work at a boot-blacking factory at the age of 12, when their father was imprisoned for bankruptcy. Dickens never forgave her when she was reluctant to remove him and send him to school, even when his father had repaid the debt.

His father was the exact opposite, a man with not a care in the world and one hundred creditors chasing his every step. A man who drifted through life bouncing from one financial crisis to the next, unable to control neither his spending nor his desire to spend.

The oil lamp in the compartment was shining brightly now. Outside the window, Manchester was getting closer and closer. In the last rays of dusk, Dickens could see the gas lights burning in the windows of the mills and the dark smoke streaming from the chimneys. Would they continue on through the night? Did they ever stop?

The train blew its whistle loudly, answered by another from somewhere far off in the forest of chimneys. The steward arrived and bowed in front of him. 'We will be arriving in London Road Station in Manchester in five minutes, Mr Dickens, sir. Will I be calling you a porter?'

'That won't be necessary, I'm being met.'

'As you wish, sir.'

The train slowed to a crawl. Outside the window, Dickens could see blackened hovels, tenements and terraced houses that clustered around the factories like piglets suckling on a farrowing sow.

The words of Dante reached out from his schooldays. 'Abandon all hope, ye who enter here.'

CHAPTER NINE

October 3, 1843
Manchester

Dickens stood at the door of the carriage, looking for his sister, hoping she had come to meet him; he longed to talk with her.

Instead, he saw the smiling face of a somebody he knew.

'Ainsworth, my good friend, how wonderful it is to see you again.'

William Harrison Ainsworth was a fellow novelist who had helped Dickens in the early days, introducing his *Sketches by Boz* to a publisher. Unfortunately, Ainsworth's last novel, *Jack Sheppard*, had been roundly condemned by the critics. And when a servant who killed his master claimed the novel had given him the idea, the same critics sat down to feast on his carcass. Three years later, his friend was still smarting from the reviews and the controversy, and their friendship had cooled considerably.

However, Dickens was happy to see him once again. A friendly face in this dour city was always welcome.

Ainsworth took his bag, handing it to a waiting porter. 'Welcome to Manchester, Dickens. I trust you had a good journey.'

'I did. It will never cease to amaze me that I was in London but nine hours ago.'

They walked together to a waiting drab yellow Hansom cab with a heraldic device painted on the door. 'I've booked you into the Adelphi again, I hope that is suitable?'

'Good, I was hoping I could stay at the same hotel as last time.'

They climbed into the cab, closing the door behind them. Ainsworth shouted their destination to the cabbie. The carriage was older and more dilapidated than those in London, the horse and cabbie both decrepit and down at heel.

The cab jerked into motion, throwing Dickens back into his seat.

Ainsworth had braced himself against the side; he was obviously more used to the driving skills of Manchester cabbies.

The noise of the cab was immense at it rattled across cobblestones, the uneven shape of which reminding Dickens of petrified kidneys.

'Now, Charles,' he shouted over the sound, 'I have been tasked with arranging your itinerary by the Athenaeum.'

'I need to spend time with Fanny. I was expecting her to be here this evening.'

'I hope you don't mind, I asked her not to come. I thought you would be fatigued by your journey.'

As ever, Ainsworth was correct. Dickens felt exhausted, every bone in his thirty-two-year-old body ached.

'But she has arranged a luncheon party in her house tomorrow, for yourself and a few guests. The day after I have kept free – I know how you like to explore – with a dinner in the evening with a few board members and the other guests, Mr Disraeli and Mr Cobden, before the speech.'

'Good.'

'Mr Watkin, the Chairman of the Athenaeum, would like to meet you beforehand to discuss some details of the soiree.'

'Perhaps he could drop in to Fanny's luncheon?'

'I will ask him.'

'Who will be coming to the soiree?'

'The great and good of Manchester as well as all those who have contributed to the building and the books. A few of the readers have been invited too.'

'I enjoy a crowd. And this evening?'

'Just a quiet supper together at the hotel.'

'Perfect. I am much obliged to you, Ainsworth.'

'Think nothing of it. Although I spend most of my days down in the capital these days, I am still keen to welcome my friends to my home city. A place that has achieved so much in such a short time.'

Dickens stared out of the carriage. On either side, warehouses and mills loomed over the street, their bright lights illuminating the way. Cutting through the constant rattle of the cab was the noise of looms, like the dull rhythmic throb of a toothache; always there, pounding the brain.

'Just a year ago these streets were full of rioters looting shops, torching factories and attacking the good men of the police,' Harrison sniffed. 'Look at them now, back at work and beavering away, the Plug Riots forgotten.'

'Plug Riots?'

'They removed the plugs from beneath the steam engines, draining all the water and thus disabling them. Hence, plug riots.'

'Attacking the machines? Why would people attack machines?'

'My dear Charles, the steam engines allow the looms to be powered, producing cottons of a quality and variety that is unsurpassed throughout the world, providing employment for all these people.'

He waved at the scene outside as they passed the entrance to a mill, a chaotic crowd of men, women and children crowding round the cast-iron gate waiting to enter.

'So why then, Ainsworth, were there riots?'

'A combination of hunger, a fifty per cent wage cut and agitation by the Chartists demanding parliamentary reform. And, of course, the events of Peterloo are still strong in many of these people's minds.'

'But now they are back at work?'

'The necessity to eat and feed a family has a great influence on a man's mind. That and two thousand troops in the city with cavalry on the corner of every major thoroughfare. People soon got the message.'

Dickens saw one man walking along, his shoulders hunched, hands in his pockets and cap pulled down over his eyes. 'Looks like they are beaten, downtrodden.'

'They are. But what to do? It is the way of the modern world.'

'But at what cost, Harrison?' he finally said. 'At what cost?'

CHAPTER TEN

Monday, December 16, 2019
Buxton Residential Home, Derbyshire

After the meeting, Jayne decided to drive to see Robert and Vera rather than visit her old pals at the Manchester nick. She would be going into town in the next week or so and could visit them before Christmas, perhaps taking in a single malt as a gift. She remembered how Sergeant McNally loved his single malts.

After a long discussion, Jayne had finally decided to take the Dickens job. As she put the car in gear and heard Bowie blasting out from the speakers, she tried to remember why.

'I'm sorry, Mr Underwood, I promised myself I would take a break before Christmas and if I take your job, I know I wouldn't be able to do that. So, unfortunately, I must decline.'

'But please, Jayne, you're our last hope.'

'You've tried other genealogists?'

Underwood looked down and spoke quietly. 'No. Another investigator.'

'That's why you're so short of time, isn't it?'

'I briefed somebody one month ago, but nothing happened. They just sat on the job and told us two days ago that they couldn't find Robert Duckworth.'

A silence descended over the table.

Finally, Ronald Welsh spoke, his eyes staring at her. 'I really would like you to do it, Mrs Sinclair. I have a good feeling about you.'

She indicated right at the end of the street and then left on to Great Ancoats Street. From here it was a relatively easy route on to the A6 to head out on the long drive to Buxton, where her dad's residential home was located.

As she remembered the conversation, she realised it was Ronald's words that had finally made up her mind. She was a sucker for 'good feelings'.

'Look,' she eventually said, 'I can give you three days' work, that's all I have free. I don't know if we can find this Robert Duckworth in that time, but that's all the time I have.'

'And that's all the time we have too, Jayne. The auction will definitely go ahead on December nineteenth, whatever happens.'

'I can't promise any results in three days...'

'We understand.' Michael Underwood coughed. 'As for payment?'

'You just need to pay my daily rate plus expenses.'

'There's a slight problem with that...'

'Which is?'

'Until the auction goes through, we don't actually have any money. But if you can discover who Robert Duckworth was, and if he has a living family, then it could add another sixty thousand pounds to the auction price. We might just have a bidding war on our hands.' He smiled and rubbed his palms together.

Ronald jumped in. 'But it's not the money that's the most important thing, is it, Mrs Sinclair? It's discovering something new. Finding out who was the inspiration for one of Dickens' most famous characters.'

Ronald understood her so well. Money was the least of her worries. 'You can pay me after the auction.'

Michael Underwood rubbed his hands again. 'Great, when will you start?'

'As soon as I can. I'd like to read *A Christmas Carol* again first, remind myself of the characters and the story. Last time I read it I was still at school.'

'You don't know what you've been missing, Mrs Sinclair. It's a wonderful story, one of my favourites from Dickens.'

And that was it. They stood up and shook hands. Michael Underwood gave her a file with photocopies of the title pages and inscriptions from the book.

Why had she said yes?

More work was the last thing she needed. What she really wanted was a break away from the past, a time to live in the present, and a plan for the future. At the moment, she had none of these and another year was nearly over. What would 2020 hold for her?

She dismissed these thoughts from her mind and concentrated on driving to Buxton. Down the A6 through Stockport and New Mills, the hills of the Pennines creeping ever closer. On either side of the road, posters from the recently completed election stood forlornly in people's gardens.

She never voted herself, believing it only encouraged politicians. As a copper, she had always been steadfastly neutral when she was policing any demonstration or rally. As a servant of the crown, it was the least she could do.

Fifty minutes later, she was parking up outside Robert and Vera's residential home. It was located in an old Victorian house in beautiful grounds. Robert had chosen it three years ago, when he had been diagnosed with early-onset Alzheimer's. Jayne had gone through anguish at the thought of being separated from him. But he had insisted. 'It's for the best, love. You have your own life to lead and here I'll get the care I need.'

'But…'

'No more ifs and buts, I've decided and that's that.'

Once Robert had made his mind up, an earthquake couldn't move him. It turned out to be the best decision he had ever made. Inside the home, he had met another resident, Vera Atkins. They had fallen in love and married. Jayne had never seen her stepfather so happy, not even when he was married to her mother. The marriage had put a spring in his step and a bounce in his heart. He looked like a brand new person.

Jayne locked the car and went into reception. 'Are they in the usual place?'

The receptionist shook her head. 'No, they're not in their corner in the TV room. You'll find them in the annex beneath the large picture window. But still doing their crosswords.'

Jayne walked through the TV room and on into the annex. Her stepfather and his wife were sitting in the corner. Vera raised her arm in greeting as soon as she saw Jayne.

'I thought you would have finished that book already.'

Her father looked up. 'You only gave us this *Guardian Book of Crosswords* last week, give us a chance.'

She bent down and kissed her father on the top of his head. 'I'm only teasing you, Dad. I know you'll have it finished by tomorrow.'

Her father held up the book.

'We've still got twelve to go, plus some of the bloody clues are still not coming together. Me and Vera have puzzled over this one for over an hour already. "Somebody who wants more has a nothing body part in return." It has six letters then five and we've got the second letter, "l", and the fourth, "v". The last letter of the second word is "t".'

Jayne looked over his shoulder at the half-completed crossword. She gave them both these books to help pass the time and because she knew it reinforced her father's belief that it exercised his brain. 'I haven't a clue, Dad, you know I'm hopeless at these things.'

'We think it probably means somebody who wants more,' said Vera, leaning into Robert, 'but we're not sure.'

And then all of a sudden, Jayne knew the answer. She smiled at her stepmother and stepfather. 'This is how it feels, does it? When you know the answer to a clue and nobody else does?'

'You've worked it out? Tell us the answer.' Robert poised his pen over the book.

Jayne stretched her neck. 'This is a nice feeling, I could get used to this very easily.'

'Don't tease an old man, love.'

She kissed his head again. 'You're not old, Robert, you just have a few years under your belt. And the answer is Oliver Twist.'

Robert stared at the book for a long time. 'She's right, you know, Vera – it is Oliver Twist. He was somebody who wanted more and the zero plus liver makes Oliver. The last bit about "in return" refers to the Twist part.'

'Well done, Jayne,' said Vera. 'We'll make you a crossword addict yet.'

Jayne laughed. 'No chance, it's just a coincidence, that's all.'

Her father looked up at her, his eyes narrowing. 'A coincidence?'

'I've just been asked to look into somebody who lived in Manchester with a possible connection to Charles Dickens.'

'That sounds interesting.'

'It is, but I've only got three days to work on it. Take a look at these.' Jayne showed the photocopies to both of them.

'But that would be wonderful, Jayne. If you could prove a connection to Manchester for this man, it would be grand.'

'It was one of my favourite books when I was young,' said Vera. 'We read it at Sunday School before every Christmas. I was even in a play about it once.'

'I can only just remember the novel. I'm going to read it again tonight.'

'Do that, love. Won't take you long, it's only a short Christmas novella.' Then a look passed between Robert and Vera. After a short pause, her father continued speaking. 'Talking about Christmas, lass, would you mind if we went up to Scotland to see Vera's relatives this year? We'd probably stay on over Hogmanay too.'

Jayne was taken aback. She always spent Christmas with Robert, and had done every year since she was a girl and her mother had married him.

For her, Robert and Christmas were one and the same.

She remembered one year – she must have been about nine or ten and her belief in Father Christmas was under threat – she had stayed awake as late as she could, listening at the door. She heard her mother talking to Robert in her usual sharp tones. 'Why do you bother dressing up in that ridiculous outfit every year? She can't see you, she's fast asleep.'

Jayne opened the door a crack. Robert was dressed as Santa Claus, putting out the presents in front of the Christmas tree he insisted on buying every year.

'It's the spirit of Christmas, love, just in case Jayne sees me. I'd like her to believe in Santa Claus for as long as she can.'

Jayne closed the door quietly and scurried into her bed. The next morning she pretended she had seen Santa Claus laying out the gifts beneath the tree.

'I told you, lass, he comes every year, just for you,' Robert had said.

'You don't mind, do you, Jayne?'

Vera's question brought her mind racing back to the present. 'Of course not, you guys please go and enjoy yourselves. Have a great time with your relatives in Scotland.'

'It's just that we won't go if you're going to be on your own, lass. We wouldn't want you to spend Christmas alone.'

Jayne found an excuse in a little white lie.

'Don't worry, Tom is taking me out. One of those posh dos where I'll have to get dressed up and wear high heels.'

She paused for a moment, thinking of her research this morning. 'How are you related to these people, Vera?'

'Through my great-uncle, Sam Duckworth. They moved up to Scotland years ago. I used to spend many happy summer days visiting them.'

'Your grandfather was Francis Duckworth, wasn't he?'

'That's right. How did you know?'

Robert coughed. 'You came across the name when you were looking for Vera's brother, didn't you, Jayne?'

'Yes... yes, I did,' she stammered.

Her father was very quick at covering for her, he knew she was working on Vera's family tree.

There was a slight pause and then her step-mother spoke. 'Talking about my brother in Australia, we're thinking of going there in late February. Get away from the winter and fly somewhere warm. What do you think, Jayne?'

'A great idea. It's a long flight but I'm sure it would be great to see Harry again.'

There was another cough from Robert. 'What Vera means is that she'd love you to join us. You've been working so hard recently, it would be lovely for you to have a break.'

Jayne thought for a moment. She'd never been to Australia, and it would be wonderful to spend some time with Vera and Robert, seeing the country. 'I don't know, Robert, I am busy at the moment—'

'All the more reason for you to have a break,' interrupted Vera. 'You could do with a holiday – and anyway, don't you have clients in Australia? You could visit them at the same time. Call it a working holiday…'

Vera was a smart woman.

'Let's decide after Christmas,' Jayne said finally.

'And you don't mind us not being here at Christmas?'

'Of course not, you both have a wonderful time in Scotland.'

'Oh, that's a relief,' said Vera, 'we were so worried about telling you.'

Jayne kissed her stepmother on the head. 'Enjoy yourselves, but don't let Robert drink too much whisky. You know it gives him ideas.'

'Aye, lass, the spirit is willing, but the flesh is weak,' said Robert over the top of his crossword book.

Jayne stayed another thirty minutes before it was time for their evening meal and for her to leave. After saying her goodbyes, she went out to the car and just sat inside for a few moments.

She knew she should be happy for them, and going to Australia together in February was an appealing idea, but a strange feeling washed over her. For a moment, she felt a strange disquiet.

She was going to spend Christmas alone.

It wasn't a happy feeling.

CHAPTER ELEVEN

Monday, December 16, 2019
Didsbury, Manchester

Jayne arrived home and was immediately greeted by a meowing Mr Smith, tail proudly held aloft, intertwining his body between her legs as she struggled out of her coat.

The weather had changed as she drove back. From quiet, almost placid, battleship-grey Manchester to a city raging and storming with sheets of ice-cold rain being blown across from Iceland. Even in the short run from her car to the front door her coat had become soaked. At least the house was just as warm and welcoming as Mr Smith.

'Okay, okay. I know you are hungry, my lord and master, I get the message.'

To reinforce his point, Mr Smith sauntered into the kitchen and sniffed his bowl as if to point out how empty it was.

Jayne switched on her computer to check messages and, while it booted up, searched for a sachet of food in the fridge for the cat. The shelves were bare except for one Lil' Grillers Tuna Special. Luckily he liked this one, although why it was called Lil' Grillers or why it was special, she had no idea.

Time to go to the supermarket again. She could go without food herself but Mr Smith had to be fed to his highness's strict dietary requirements. In other words, expensive cat food.

She poured a little dry kibble in the bowl, topping it with the wet chunks of tuna. Mr Smith pounced immediately, as if he hadn't eaten for the last week, crouching down and lapping up the wet food followed by the crunch of the dry.

Jayne thought about opening her emails and then changed her mind. Time to open a nice bottle instead. The news that her parents were going to Scotland for Christmas had disturbed her more than she cared to admit. Of course, she was happy for them, but it was a tradition that she cooked Christmas dinner for them both.

At least, it was a tradition in her mind, having started two years ago after she had split up with Paul, her ex-husband. They were now officially divorced and he was engaged to a twenty-three-year-old Belgian beauty therapist, whatever one of those was. He had even invited her to his wedding in February in Brussels. But her chance of going was about the same as Rochdale winning the World Cup. In other words, none.

It wasn't that she was bitter about the break-up. On the contrary, she saw it as inevitable. They had just drifted apart as he became more and more wrapped up in his job and she devoted her time to her genealogical investigations.

She would always be grateful for his support of her during the most difficult time in her life. When, as a detective, she had made a routine check on a house in Moss Side. Her partner, Dave Gilmour, had knocked on the door while she had leant on the wall to one side, chatting aimlessly about something or other. The shots, when they came, exploded through the door, hitting her partner in the chest. The last words she remembered hearing from his blood-stained mouth were, 'I should have ducked… Rookie mistake.'

He had died in her arms.

It took a long while to get over his death. When she returned to the police three months later, after counselling, it just wasn't the same any more. It was as if her whole career had been tainted.

Could she have acted differently? Could she have prevented his death? Couldn't she have guessed what was going to happen?

Nobody blamed her, but she blamed herself.

A shudder ran down her spine. 'Don't think about it now, Jayne. Not now.'

Mr Smith looked up from his bowl for a second before returning to a particularly appetising piece of soggy tuna. Jayne took out a nice bottle of Sagrantino from Montefalco and poured herself a large glass, smelling the aroma and drinking a large gulp, feeling the warm hug of an Italian summer circle around her mouth.

She thought about answering her emails, or even starting to search for the family of Robert Duckworth in the 1841 Census. But she was tired, and even though she had only three days to find the answer, she knew starting now as a mistake. Being so tired, all she would do was miss important clues or hints that she should follow up.

And then it struck her what she had to do. She put her wine glass down and rushed into the living room. It was a place she only used occasionally; most of the time she spent in the kitchen. She had created her whole life there, so everything she needed from her work files to her computer to a glass of wine were always close at hand.

In the living room, she looked at the bookshelves in the corner. 'It must be here somewhere,' she said out loud, 'I knew I put it here.' And then she saw it, nestled between an Ian Rankin crime thriller and *Winnie the Pooh*.

She reached up and pulled out the thin volume from the shelf.

A Christmas Carol by Charles Dickens.

Opening the book, she saw the inscription written inside. 'To Jayne from Mum, Happy Christmas '92.'

It was a time when they still got on, before her teenage rebellion turned into outright war. Her mum always gave her five presents every Christmas, and in 1992 this book was one of them. It was a Penguin edition and the pages were slightly yellowing now.

She flicked to the title page. It was a copy of the first edition she had seen that morning in the café. A couple of the pages were folded back in dog-ears where Jayne had marked the point when she had finished reading, all those years ago.

A bright twelve year old, but one who was deeply troubled by the absence of her father and the constant feeling she had somehow disappointed her mother.

Luckily, her step-father Robert had been there to be her rock; she didn't know what she would have done without him.

She went back into the kitchen to retrieve her wine. Mr Smith was lazily licking his white paws, having demolished the bowl of food.

'No more until tomorrow,' she announced.

He ignored her, continuing with the far more important task of making sure his feet were clean before he embarked on his evening prowl down to number nine.

She was sure her neighbour was also feeding him, but she wasn't certain and Mr Smith wasn't telling.

She returned to the living room and settled down in the comfort of her armchair, opening the book to read the preface.

I have endeavoured in this Ghostly little book, to raise the Ghost of an Idea, which shall not put my readers out of humour with themselves, with each other, with the season, or with me. May it haunt their houses pleasantly, and no one wish to lay it.

Their faithful Friend and Servant,

C. D.

CHAPTER TWELVE

Monday, December 16, 2019
Didsbury, Manchester

Three hours later, with the bottle of Sagrantino finished, she finally laid the book down.

The story had come back to her in the reading.

The meanness and greed of Ebenezer Scrooge. The arrival of Marley's ghost to warn Scrooge about the error of his ways. Looking back with the Ghost of Christmas Past to see Scrooge's unhappy childhood and his lost love for Belle. The Ghost of Christmas Present showing him how the Cratchits, the Fezziwigs and his nephew Fred's family enjoyed Christmas, despite having far less money than him. Finally, the Ghost of Christmas to Come showing the awfulness of the future, with nobody mourning his demise and Tiny Tim dying a slow and painful death.

But Dickens didn't end *A Christmas Carol* on a depressing note. He showed that renewal and renaissance were possible if only one treated their fellow man with dignity and humanity. Everybody, even Ebenezer Scrooge, was capable of change.

It struck Jayne that this wasn't just a Christmas story, but one for any time of the year. A story of humanity and hope, of sharing and selflessness. Perhaps that was why it was so universally loved.

She looked at the book again. Had her mother been trying to tell her something with this present? But in her self-absorbed early teens, Jayne wouldn't have been able to see the message let alone understand it.

She remembered the dedication on the front leaf of the edition discovered by Ronald Welsh.

To my friend, Robert Duckworth, and his son, of Manchester, a Christmas Present for showing me a Christmas Past and a Christmas yet to come.

Who was Robert Duckworth? Was he really from Manchester? How had he shown Dickens about the Ghosts of Christmas? And more importantly, did his family still exist?

If they were still alive, Jayne was sure she would be able to find them.

She remembered her research into Vera's ancestors from this morning. Could this Robert Duckworth be related to her stepmother? The odds would be fantastic, but still, the identical surname was a link.

She stood up, yawned, stretched and took the now empty bottle and glass back through to the kitchen.

Mr Smith was waiting patiently in front of the patio door. Outside, the rain was still beating against the glass, the wind howling as if all the Ghosts of Christmas were desperate to be let into the house.

'Are you sure you want to go out?' she asked the cat.

She opened the door slightly and he rushed out into the dark. 'Rather you than me,' she said as he vanished from view.

She stood there for a few seconds, the wind blowing through her hair, feeling the icy rain on her face, wishing for one short breath that she could share this moment with somebody, anybody.

Then she shook her head, dismissed the thought and closed the patio door. She looked at her computer and decided she would start the research early tomorrow morning.

Could she find Robert Duckworth? She hoped so.

For some reason, after reading *A Christmas Carol*, it mattered to her now.

It would be her gift to Christmas.

CHAPTER THIRTEEN

October 3, 1843
The Adelphi Hotel, Manchester

Dickens slipped beneath the sheets of his bed. The room was spartan yet comfortable, reminding him of the rooms in which he had spent much of his life as a parliamentary reporter, quickly dashing off sketches of the debates and the proceedings.

It had been a long day, too long. Beside his bed, next to the wash basin and water jug from some factory in the Potteries, a lone candle burnt, its flame flickering in the draught from the door.

Dickens lay back and tried to sleep but his thoughts crowded in his mind. What should he do about *Chuzzlewit*? How could he make the serial more enjoyable for his readers? A twist in the tail? A long-lost orphan or a forgotten sister?

Perhaps, but it all seemed so contrived, so melodramatic.

And what about his finances? The statement from Coutts had disturbed him greatly. Catherine was no use in these matters and since she had become pregnant with their fifth child, even less involved in day-to-day affairs, neglecting their existing family. She left all the finances to him, rightfully so. It was a man's job to provide for his family. A duty in which his father had singularly failed throughout his life.

His father. Another begging letter and more money needed to redeem his debts. Where did the man spend the money? It wasn't on anything tangible – Dickens had seen his clothes, they looked as if they belonged more in the tatter's yard than on his father's back.

More expense.

Perhaps he should take Somerfield's advice and find another publisher. Chapman & Hall had not publicised Chuzzlewit at all; no wonder the serial was failing. They seemed to take so much money for doing far too little. Should he take his solicitor's advice and change publishers? The contract was execrable, he knew that, signed when he was a young whippersnapper desperate to have a book in print. But now he was famous, selling well and worth a lot more.

His dinner with Ainsworth had been revealing. The Athenaeum speech was more important than he thought. The great and good of Manchester society would be there to greet the 'famous author', as his friend had described him with more than a touch of irony, or was it jealousy?

'It's more than a soiree in support of a library, Charles, it's a focus away from their obsession with facts, facts, facts as the source of everything that is good and true. I believe it's the beginning of an understanding that there is more to life than toil and labour and profit. That art and learning may be just as essential in modern life.'

Dickens had re-read his speech before retiring. It was anodyne at best and patronising at worst, saying nothing except the expected. It would have to be re-written yet again. When would he find the time?

A creak of the floorboards. The candle flickered briefly and went out.

Dickens listened for a while.

Another creak.

'Who's there?' he shouted. 'Show yourself.'

He stared into the dark, waiting for a response. Was somebody here to rob him? Or worse, murder him in his bed?

'Who's there?' he shouted again.

No answer.

Outside, in the far distance, he could hear the steady throb of the steam engines pounding away in the mills. Did they never stop working?

He thought about going for a walk. It was his habit in London to walk the streets late at night, looking for inspiration in the lanes and alleys of his youth. Sometimes, he would walk fifteen or even twenty miles if the muse guided him. He enjoyed walking alone, his thoughts and ideas as his only company, the streets, courts and alleys his theatre, the inhabitants the cast of players.

But here, he knew nowhere to go. The dark satanic mills scared him. Perhaps he could ask Ainsworth to guide him? Not tonight then, but perhaps tomorrow, when he had summoned up enough courage, he would walk.

He lay half awake for the rest of the night, waiting for the ghost or whoever it was who had made the noise.

But nobody came.

Not that night.

CHAPTER FOURTEEN

Tuesday, December 17, 2019
Didsbury, Manchester

Jayne woke up early the following morning with a slight headache. Inwardly she criticised herself for finishing a whole bottle of wine the previous evening. She always believed wine should be for enjoyment, not merely getting drunk. But sitting in the living room, in front of a fire and reading the book, she had drunk far more than she intended.

It was a very pleasant evening, but she resolved to lay off the booze that day. It would be good for her liver and kidneys and even better for her soul.

She dressed in sweatpants and a t-shirt and tottered downstairs. Mr Smith was sat in the corner, licking his paws again, a contented purr shaking his body.

'And what time did you come in last night?' she asked him as she switched on her Nespresso machine and selected the strongest capsule she had.

There was no answer. He simply stopped what he was doing and strolled over to his empty bowl and stared at it mournfully.

'Whatever it was, you're obviously starving.' Then Jayne remembered there was no wet cat food left. She took out the dry food from the cupboard and emptied a good cupful into Mr Smith's bowl. 'This will have to do until I get to the supermarket.'

The cat looked at his bowl, sniffed twice, then looked back at her, before strolling off to his favourite windowsill in the hall, tail erect.

'Please yourself.' The aroma of coffee filled the kitchen. Jayne took the cup and switched on her computer.

'Where to begin?' she asked herself, deciding almost immediately to dive right in. She opened the Findmypast website and selected the 1841 Census for England and Wales. She typed in 'Robert Duckworth' with no filters. She didn't know his birth date or even how old he was.

168 results.

Not great. She added the filter for Lancashire, as that was the county for Manchester in the 1840s.

136 results.

A sinking feeling struck Jayne. This wasn't going to be as straightforward as she thought. She checked on the Forebears website. Duckworth was the 20,722nd most common surname in the world.

Not bad, but not great either. Surname regularity always affected every search. Luckily, the man she was looking for wasn't called Smith or Davies or Evans.

She dug a little further. In England, the surname was ranked 1274th and had an incidence of 6338. She scrolled down to check the name's origin. Duckworth was derived from a geographical locality ' —of Duckworth— ' an estate in Oswaldtwistle, a township in the parish of Whalley, Lancashire.

The name actually originated only thirty miles north of Manchester. But given there was far less mobility back in 1841, she hoped the number of people with that combination of surname and Christian name in Manchester was low. Perhaps even Vera's ancestors had come from the same locality.

Jayne added the filter for Manchester and just 15 results came back. She heaved a sigh of relief. At least that number was manageable, with the big proviso that when Dickens wrote 'of Manchester' in 1843, he was referring to Robert Duckworth living there.

She scanned down the list. Of the fifteen Robert Duckworths, four were born after 1828. In his dedication, Dickens had referred to his 'good friend'. Would one refer to a child like that?

Probably not.

She was then left with eleven names, with births ranging from 1801 to 1826. She checked the 1841 Census again, bringing out her notebook to write in a list of possibilities.

She clicked on the first name and saw the Census listing.

Birth	Address	Family	Job	Resident
1801	Minshull St	Mary, 5 children	Twister	St James Ward

She opened another website to check the job. The cotton industry in Manchester had many strange job names and titles.

A 'twister' was somebody who 'joins the ends of a fresh beam of threads on to the warp already on the loom. A sitting-down job, sometimes done by people who were crippled'.

Interesting, the job could have been done by somebody who was handicapped. She thought back to Tiny Tim in the novel. Was this a possible link with *A Christmas Carol*?

She checked with the Census.

There was no mention of a disability but that wasn't unusual. Such notes weren't added to the Census until 1851, and even then it was limited to deafness, blindness, the inability to speak or whether or not the person was a lunatic or an inmate at an asylum. It was up to the individual enumerator exactly what he wrote down in his Census papers.

Jayne made a note and decided to carry on researching all the rest.

She knew it would take her a long time, but it, had to be done properly if it was done at all. Now was the time to dig deep.

Birth	Address	Family	Job	Resident
1801	Minshull St	Mary, 5 children	Twister	St James Ward
1806	Adam Rd	Eliza, 4 children	Calico Printer	Angel Meadow
1807	????	Mary, 2 children	Tailor	College Ward
1811	Mill St	Sarah, 2 children	Cotton Weaver	Ancoats

1816	Howard Lane	Sarah, no children	Power Loom Operator	Stockp't
1816	Ardwick Green	Helen, 5 children	Block Printer	Ardwick
1819	Newberry St	Mary, 2 children	Clerk	St Annes
1826	Tickle Lane	Single	Back Tender	St John
1826	Dover St	Single	None	Chorlton-on-M
1826	St John's St	Single	None	Crumpsall
1826	Hanging Ditch	Single	None	Deansgate

By three o' clock, she had written down all the Robert Duckworths; their birth date, address, family, job and area of residence.

Jayne glanced over her notes. Nothing stood out as strikingly obvious that they were the person to whom Dickens had dedicated the book.

She recognised the names of the suburbs and districts of Manchester such as Stockport, Ardwick and Deansgate, these places still existed.

107

Chorlton-on-M was the short form for Chorlton-on-Medlock, an area close to the city centre, just south of Oxford Road. The name was rarely used any more, even though Jayne often saw it on older documents.

She checked out the inscription in the book again. It mentioned Robert Duckworth and a son.

Did that mean she could eliminate the single men? She felt that was an acceptable assumption given the lack of time to investigate everybody who appeared on the list.

After that, her tally was now reduced to just seven possibilities.

Birth	Address	Family	Job	Residence
1801	Minshull St	Mary, 5 children	Twister	St James Ward
1806	Adam Rd	Eliza, 4 children	Calico Printer	Angel Meadow
1807	????	Mary, 2 children	Tailor	College Ward
1811	Mill St	Sarah, 2 children	Cotton Weaver	Ancoats

1816	Howard Lane	Sarah, no children	Power Loom Operator	Stockp't
1816	Ardwick Green	Helen, 5 children	Block Printer	Ardwick
1819	Newberry St	Mary, 2 children	Clerk	St Annes

Time to quickly check out the 1851 Census for Manchester. She knew there were problems with these documents but she had to look at them. She typed in the name and pressed send. A note immediately appeared, stating that many records for the city's Census had been damaged or destroyed. Jayne clicked on one of the links anyway.

The image was totally illegible.

'Bugger,' she said. Mr Smith looked at her as if offended by her language.

'Sorry,' she apologised.

He went back to sleep.

She went to her bookshelf and found a note she had written about the 1851 Census. 'Family historians with ancestors in mid-19th century Manchester face a particular difficulty. Following the transfer of the enumeration books to the Home Office in London and an analysis of the contents, the area where the books were stored was flooded and the books were badly damaged. Some of the books were in such poor condition that it was not considered worth filming them. Others were filmed but much of the image appears blackened and the writing is not decipherable. The following areas are completely missing: Blackley, Harpurhey, and Moston, along with parts of Hulme, St George's and London Road districts. Much of the Census for Deansgate, Ardwick and Chorlton-on-Medlock area is also completely illegible.'

That was exactly how she remembered it.

She checked the details of her Robert Duckworths. Most lived in the areas affected.

A previous case, however, had given her a way round this problem. It wasn't completely foolproof but it was better than nothing.

The volunteers at the Manchester and Lancashire Family History Society had done a lot of work to retrieve information on these areas, accessing the damaged returns and transcribing them. Despite the damage, details of some 82% of the 217,717 persons whom the statisticians had counted had been transcribed.

She went back to her computer and entered the address for the 'Unfilmed' website. A simple search page popped up with the transcribed returns. It might not be totally accurate, but it was better than nothing.

She compared the two lists of names, putting red crosses against three that were missing from the Census in 1851, confirming two others had moved house, and adding three new people to her list, two of which were born in 1826, suggesting the singles had married.

The new list had now lengthened unfortunately.

Birth	Address	Family	Job	Residence
1801	Minshull St	Mary, 5 children	Twister	St James Ward XXX
1806	Rogers Rd	Eliza, 4 children	Calico Printer	Angel Meadow
1807	????	Mary, 2 children	Tailor	College Ward XXX
1811	Minehead St	Sarah, 2 children	Cotton Weaver	Ancoats
1816	Howard Lane	Sarah, no children	Power Loom Operator	Stockport XXX
1816	Ardwick Green	Helen, 5 children	Block Printer	Ardwick

1819	New-berry St	Mary, 2 children	Clerk	St Annes
1817	Halson St	Mary, 4 children	Editor	Chorlton-on-M
1826	Plymouth Grove	Eliza, 3 children	Fustian Shearer	Ardwick
1826	Hanging Ditch	Emily, 2 children	Clerk	Deansgate

She still needed to check out all ten names. Perhaps more, if her Robert Duckworth was on the 18% of returns for 1851 that couldn't be transcribed. Or perhaps he had moved away. Or maybe he had just been missed by the enumerator.

She sat in front of the computer and scratched her head.

Ten names was far too many. Any of the people here could have been the book's owner.

Or none of them.

That was the problem. There was just too little information to work with.

She needed to focus in on the period from 1841 to the end of 1843, when she knew Robert Duckworth was living in Manchester.

The documents did exist. Unfortunately, it involved another trip into the city. To the local studies section of Manchester Central Library, to be precise.

But that would have to wait until tomorrow, as it was too late to traipse all the way into town now. Besides, she wanted to check her research so far. Too often mistakes were made and they caused problems further down the line. Jayne was meticulous in making sure her research was accurate.

Would she be able to solve this mystery in time?

The truth was, she didn't know.

CHAPTER FIFTEEN

October 4, 1843
The Adelphi Hotel, Manchester

Dickens woke the next morning, tired and irritable.

He had hardly slept, tossing and turning most of the night, missing his comfortable bed at home in London, Catherine's gentle snores beside him a comforting rhythmic sound.

He rose and breakfasted downstairs. A glorious affair of cold hams, venison pies, suet puddings, ham and eggs, kippers, Easterhedge pudding – a concoction of sorrel, nettles and barley mixed with eggs and butter – fresh breads, creams, curds and marmalades, served with a pot of hot coffee in the American style and a glass of Madeira as a digestif.

The middle class of Manchester at least knew how to eat well. He felt better, ready to meet his darling sister and face the day.

He returned upstairs and dressed, choosing a bright yellow silk waistcoat and matching it with a large sky-blue overcoat with bright red cuffs. He did like to look his best when he met his sister and her children. Even more, the bright colours would no doubt offend the susceptibilities of his puritan brother-in-law, Henry. A man he never minded upsetting.

He took one last look in the mirror and pronounced himself satisfied. One should always make a show for one's audience; he believed, along with his beloved Shakespeare, that life was but a stage and he was a mere player upon it.

Taking out a parcel from his carpetbag, he placed it in a paisley satchel he had borrowed from the innkeeper. The children would be amused by his new profession. He hoped so after all the long hours he had put in practising.

He rushed downstairs and called for a carriage, slinging the bag inside when it arrived. 'Three Elm Terrace, Higher Ardwick,' he called up to the driver.

'That'll be one shilling and sixpence, guvnor. It's on the edge of the city.'

'Just take me there.'

'As your honour desires,' the cabbie grumbled, clicking his tongue to encourage the horse to trot on. The carriage rumbled forward, bouncing up and down on the cobbles,. The springs seemed to be absent or nor longer functioning.

Outside, the mills still rumbled, rattled, hooted and boomed as they had been doing all day and night. Children no older than three or four ran barefoot through the muddy puddles, running alongside his coach for a moment, their hands held high in the air.

Dickens ignored them. Experience had told him that if he gave one boy money, soon there would be a veritable army of followers and his carriage would be a pied piper leading a long stream of waifs.

He believed in charity, but it must be effective. The simple doling-out of money was not the answer.

On his right, a whistle blew from the top of a dark, soot-blackened chimney.

Within seconds, a gang of women, children and a few men rushed out, surrounding the hawkers who had gathered outside the mill gates, shouting out their wares: hot potatoes, bowls of thin gruel, bread soaked in warmed milk, steaming urns of tea. Workers clustered around the hawkers, quickly grabbing something to eat or drink before their break was over.

Dickens suddenly felt tired. He closed his eyes and listened to the sounds of the city all around him; the rattle of the carriage, the sharp peep of the factory whistles, the constant, deep throb of the steam engines. The noises of industry, red in tooth and claw.

Gradually, the harsh grating sounds gave way to something softer, more rural; the rustle of wind through leaves, the soft clop of the horse's hooves against compacted earth, the chime of a church bell.

'We is here,' the cabbie announced.

Dickens popped his head out of the small window. The door of the house opened and Fanny rushed out to greet him.

'Charles, how wonderful to see you.'

He bent down and kissed his sister on the cheek. 'It's even more of a delight to see you, dear Fan.' He stepped back and held her at arm's length. 'You look well. Manchester seems to agree with you.'

He spotted his brother-in-law, Henry, standing behind his sister. 'Burnett, how wonderful to see you,' he said warmly, despite feeling absolutely no warmth for his brother-in-law. Hadn't the man's ridiculously puritan religious sensibilities stopped his sister from performing in the opera?

'How was America?' asked Henry.

'Full of Americans, but despite that, generally enjoyable. An amazingly energetic place, there is much the Old World can learn from the New.'

'I enjoyed reading *American Notes*.'

'Unfortunately, the Americans enjoyed it less. They objected to my comments on slavery.'

Fanny took his arm and began leading him to the open door. 'There are some people we'd like you to meet.' She leant in and whispered in his ear, 'Music and singing clients and the local Unitarian vicar and his wife. When they heard you were coming, they wanted to meet the great author. They support us so much, we could not say no. Also a Mr Watkin from the Athenaeum is dropping by later to discuss the arrangements for your speech.'

'I was hoping to spend some time with you and the children.'

'Later,' she said, leading him into the hallway where a line of people waited to greet him.

'May I present Mr Silas Grindley, one of our great supporters,' she began.

'Your sister has a wonderful voice, Mr Dickens, it seems the whole family is talented.'

'I'm afraid my talents stretch to the twisting of words, Mr Grindley. It is my sister who is the true artiste.'

'But what words and such characters. I never laughed so much at Sam.' He imitated Sam's accent, twisting his own northern vowels to achieve the right effect. '"I never heerd... nor read of nor see in picters, any angel in tights and gaiters... but he's a reg'lar thoroughbred angel for all that." You caught the man's voice to perfection, sir.'

'Thank you, Mr Grindley, I aim to please.'

'Bah humbug, man, you do far more than that. You educate, that's what you do. "There are very few moments in a man's existence when he experiences so much ludicrous distress, or meets with so little charitable commiseration, as when he is in pursuit of his own hat." Capital, my good fellow, capital.'

Fanny moved him along to the next man in line.

'Herbert Packet at your disposal, a humble physician.'

'We laymen are often humbled at the knowledge of the human body displayed by a physician, Mr Packet.'

'I would that it were always true, Mr Dickens. Why only—'

Another man stepped forward, interrupting Mr Packet. 'The Reverend William Gaskell at your disposal, sir. It is an honour to meet a fellow Unitarian.'

Dickens had been spending a great deal of time since his return from America with Edward Tagart at the Unitarian church on Little Portland Street in London. It seemed to him a far more accepting brotherhood than the official church.

Dickens shook his hand.

'And may I present my wife, Mrs Elizabeth Gaskell. I'm afraid she has some pretensions to join your profession.'

'You are a writer, Mrs Gaskell?'

The woman reddened, glancing at her husband. 'I have a written a few articles and short stories.'

'You should send me them. Magazines in London are always looking out for new voices.'

Next in line was a thin, ascetic man staring through pince-nez perched on the end of his nose. 'Thomas Caulfield, editor of the *Courier*, sir,' he said stiffly.

'Ah, my former profession. I hope your paper is doing well?'

'As well as can be expected given the troubled times, Mr Dickens.'

Finally, a round, fat, sweating man presented himself. 'Micawber, your servant, Mr Dickens. It is a pleasure to meet you.'

'And what do you do in this town, Mr Micawber?'

'I lend money to those who need it and can pay it back. A banker, sir.'

'Ah, it is the paying back that is the issue, isn't it, Mr Micawber, not the needing of money?'

'You understand my profession well, sir.'

'Please go through, Charles, we have a light luncheon for you and our guests,' said Fanny, guiding him towards the front room.

'We calls it dinner round here, Mrs Burnett. If you are to live in our glorious city, you need to get used to our ways,' said the banker, walking with Dickens into the room.

The light luncheon consisted of mutton and veal three ways, a brace of woodcocks, a pair of Moffat ducks swimming in their own fat, pots of braised eels, a selection of vegetables which few people had the temerity to try, a ragout of celery and, for dessert, apples, pears and chestnuts accompanied by a whole Stilton cheese, blackcurrant jelly and a lemon fool.

When all the courses had been served, Dickens sat back and opened the bottom two buttons of his waistcoat.

'I swear, Fanny, when I return to London, the railway will charge me double for the amount of weight I have put on.'

'Aye, we know how to eat well in Manchester,' said Mr Grindley. 'In my mill, we've put in a canteen so my operatives can eat their lunch.'

'I saw on my way here, workers surrounding hawkers, all trying to get something. It gladdens me that you treat your workers so well. I saw the mills in Lowell in America, and they—'

'It is not about "treating them well" as you say, sir,' Grindley interrupted. 'It is more efficient for the operatives to stay in the factory during a break. They can be back at their machines on time. It is a fact that a healthy worker is an efficient worker.'

'And it is also a fact that you make money from providing the meals, don't you, Mr Grindley?' said Mr Caulfield.

'We do, sir, and I am proud of it. You don't get owt for nowt in this city. I run my mill efficiently and based on science. Facts are all that matter, sir. If it can be measured, it can be improved. I have little time when it comes to feelings. Feelings don't pay the rent.'

'And yet you support my brother-in-law in his musical endeavours. Is not the power of music a "feeling"?' asked Dickens as politely as he could.

'I do support Mr Burnett, and gladly, but my motives have a factual basis, a utilitarian foundation.'

'And what are they?' asked the physician.

'Two reasons, sir. Firstly, my workers must enjoy some culture, they cannot live on work alone. It keeps them amused during their leisure hours. And secondly, Manchester is a great city, the centre of cotton production in England and the world. Why, last year, my own factory exported cotton goods as far afield as Chinee and the Indies. So you see, sir, we must maintain our leadership in the Arts as well as Industry. Our reputation depends on it. Otherwise, we might lose out to our neighbours to the West. I speak of the city of Liverpool, sir.'

'And what of the riots last year. Have they ceased?'

'The militia soon put them down. The rioters were nothing but agitators, saboteurs and infiltrators, all of them. The Charter is a simple blueprint for chaos and anarchy.'

Mr Micawber, the banker, coughed. 'For the last few years, the price of bread has risen and there were fewer markets for Manchester's cotton, therefore wages declined. The situation for a worker can be simply put: annual income – twenty pounds; annual expenditure – nineteen nineteen and six; result – happiness. Annual income – twenty pounds; annual expenditure – twenty pounds ought and six; result – misery.'

'You simplify too much, sir,' said Mr Grindley. 'Facts, facts, facts are all that should matter. And the inescapable fact is that when cotton is doing well, Manchester is happy. When cotton is doing badly, Manchester inevitably suffers.'

'True, sir, but what of the education of your workers?' asked William Gaskell. 'Surely if they are to improve their lot in life that can only come about through the improvement of their learning.'

'Bah humbug, sir, a little learning is a dangerous thing. And it becomes more dangerous when it is delivered by the likes of Mr Caulfield there at his Hall of Science.'

'I must disagree, sir,' protested Dickens, 'I—'

Fanny clapped her hands. 'Enough disputation, gentlemen. I feel it is time for some entertainment. I think you start, Charles, by showing us your magical tricks.'

'You are a magician, sir?' asked Mr Grindley.

'I dabble.'

'Nonsense. Charles is very good.'

Dickens held his hands up. 'I did happen to bring my magical tools with me today. But I will only agree to perform my tricks if Fanny agrees to be my assistant along with her son, Harry.'

Fanny frowned for a moment before agreeing, telling the maid, 'Bring Harry and his brother to join us.'

While the boys were brought down, Dickens brought his tools out of the bag; a magic wand, a top hat, a deck of cards and some porcelain cups. 'I have only brought those things I could easily carry.' After Fanny had cleared the table, he set them out in order.

The boys arrived and Dickens greeted them warmly. Harry was four years old, carried into the dining room by the maid as his body was still weak and undeveloped, his face a sickly yellow. Charles, the younger child, was already heavier and more active. He struggled to break free from his nanny's arms.

Harry was placed in a chair next to Dickens. 'It is good to see you, Uncle Charles,' he said softly.

'And it is even better to see you, Harry.' Dickens bent down and whispered in the boy's ear, 'Just follow my lead and all will be well.'

'I'll try my best,' he coughed.

'Ladies and gentlemen, we are here today to see a wonderful display of the magical arts from your humble servant and his assistant, the young master Harry Burnett.'

Fanny led the assembled guests in a round of cheering and clapping.

Dickens reached into his pocket. 'Would you say you are a rich man, Harry?'

'I do not think so, sir.'

'Do you think you are as rich as Mr Micawber, the banker?'

Harry eyed the guest suspiciously. 'I don't think I am, sir.'

Dickens' hand swooped out behind the boy's head. 'I beg to differ.' Suddenly he produced a gold dollar from the boy's ear. 'I think you are, Harry.'

And then he produced another, and another and another, finally giving five gold coins to the boy. 'Indeed, I think you have a head for business and the gift of making money.'

Everybody clapped and cheered. From his seat Mr Grindley said, 'See, you're a proper Mancunian now, young Master Burnett. You make money with your noggin.'

Harry blushed a deep crimson red.

Dickens produced a bright green handkerchief from his pocket. 'Please open wide, Harry.' He put the handkerchief in the boy's mouth, closing his jaws gently. Then he tapped the boy's head with his magic wand, said 'Abracadabra' three times, and reached into the boy's mouth, pulling out a white handkerchief, followed by a pink one and a blue one. A yellow polka-dotted silk square was next, while some handsome orange fabric in the shape of a string of bunting was the last to be removed.

Dickens then showed both sides of the blue handkerchief, before seemingly threading it through the boy's ear and pulling it out the other side. All this time, Harry smiled and continued to stare at his audience.

Dickens pulled the handkerchief out and displayed it to his audience, saying, 'As you see, young Harry needed his ears waxed.'

The applause was thunderous.

'You are uncommonly good, sir,' shouted Mr Grindley. 'Where did you learn your tricks?'

'These are not tricks, but magic performed by myself and my apprentice conjurer, Master Burnett.'

There followed a dazzling array of magic, prestidigitations and sleight of hand. Stuffed pigeons appeared from top hats, coins dropped into glasses, pencils vanished, and a cup overflowed with money, spilling coins on to the tablecloth.

'We'll make a banker of you yet, Mr Dickens,' shouted Mr Micawber.

'As long as you don't make a bankrupt of me, sir, I will be happy.'

The final trick involved Harry being carried out of the room and correctly guessing, each time, under which cup the coin was hidden when he returned.

'You'll be a policeman, young Harry.'

'Or a finder of treasure?' said his father.

The boy beamed from ear to ear and just as suddenly, the grin dissolved into a large yawn.

'I fear performing magic has tired him out nearly as much as it has exhausted me,' said Dickens.

His sister clapped her hands to attract everyone's attention. 'Before Harry and Charlie are taken to bed, we would like to perform a song for you. And because we know how much you love Christmas, Charles, it will be a carol – an old carol.'

Henry Burnett stepped forward and was joined by the family; a seat was found for Harry at the centre of the small choir. The nanny who looked after Charlie sat down at the pianoforte and began to play.

Charles recognised the tune immediately. It was something they used to sing when he was growing up in Chatham, a song that always brought back memories of Christmas, New Year and Twelfth Night, of cake and happiness and joy.

Here we come a-wassailing
Among the leaves so green,
Here we come a-wand'ring
So fair to be seen.
Love and joy come to you,
And to you your wassail, too,
And God bless you, and send you
A Happy New Year,
And God send you a Happy New Year.

A maid was handing out the lyrics and Fanny was encouraging people to join in the verses. Dickens sang out in his deep baritone while, on his left, Mr Micawber was singing off-key. Fanny's voice was as pure as ever, though, a joy to listen to again.

We are not daily beggars
That beg from door to door,
But we are neighbours' children

Whom you have seen before.
Love and joy come to you,
And to you your wassail, too,
And God bless you, and send you
A Happy New Year,
And God send you a Happy New Year.

Good master and good mistress,
As you sit beside the fire,
Pray think of us poor children
Who wander in the mire.
Love and joy come to you,
And to you your wassail, too,
And God bless you, and send you
A Happy New Year,
And God send you a Happy New Year!

'Congratulations, Mr and Mrs Burnett, that was most enjoyable,' gushed Silas Grindley. 'Might we not trouble you for another song?'

Harry's eyes were closing and he almost fell of his chair. Fanny rushed to lift her child off the seat and carry him upstairs. 'He is not well, gentlemen. I will take him back to his room.'

When Fanny had gone, Dickens sat back down in his chair, sweat glistening his forehead.

'A glass to you, sir, you have a fine voice. Your talents are wasted in the world of literature, they should be employed in the theatre,' said the banker.

Dickens drank his glass of hock. 'I am going tonight to the Theatre Royal to see Hamlet.'

'It is uncommonly good, sir. Mr Wilkins is a triumph.'

'I am looking forward to it.'

Grindley turned to Dickens. 'After such a performance, you should visit my mill, sir. I'm sure you would appreciate the magic of my looms.'

'I should like that very much. I visited the mills in Lowell, Massachusetts, and enjoyed seeing the happiness of the workers there very much.'

'I doubt you will see much happiness in Mr Grindley's mills,' muttered the editor.

'But you will see efficiency, and efficiency creates happiness, does it not? Shall we say eleven o'clock tomorrow, Mr Dickens?'

'That will be perfect.'

'I will send my carriage to your hotel. It is the Adelphi, is it not?'

'You are well informed, sir.'

'And you should see the other side of Manchester, too,' interrupted Elizabeth Gaskell, speaking for the first time.

'What other side is that?' asked Dickens.

'A side mill-owners like Mr Grindley would prefer to keep hidden in the courts and back streets of our city,' said Caulfield, emptying his glass of Madeira.

Silas Grindley leant forward. 'I'm afraid myself and Mr Caulfield do not see eye to eye on the subject of our city. He and his paper are all for Chartism – isn't that true, sir?'

'I am in favour of universal suffrage. That is correct.'

'Bah humbug, sir, why should anybody have a vote unless they have a stake in society? The ownership of property gives you a desire to see the correct policies implemented. Giving everyone the vote could see the rise of populism with all its problems. An unscrupulous man could promise people anything merely to get elected. No, sir, such a system is neither efficient nor welcome. Next you'll be talking about giving women and the feeble the vote.'

'And why not?' asked Mrs Gaskell. 'Are not women part of society?'

Fanny returned to the room. 'Gentlemen, gentlemen, please keep your voices down. The children are just falling asleep.'

'Our apologies, Mrs Burnett,' said Mrs Gaskell. She turned to Dickens. 'I'm afraid myself and my husband are otherwise engaged tomorrow. But I will send one of our congregation in my place to guide you through the city if you like. I believe you like walking?'

'It is my favourite pastime, madam.'

'A walking tour of Manchester then. My friend will be your guide. I will ask him to be at Grindley's mill at three p.m. Does that suit, sir?'

'It suits me well. And your friend's name?'

'Mr Robert Duckworth, a man born in this city.'

CHAPTER SIXTEEN

Tuesday, December 17, 2019
Didsbury, Manchester

Jayne had finished checking and re-checking her research, trying to make the names, addresses and dates for Robert Duckworth talk to her.

She had been back to the inscription again and again, looking for a clue in the message from Dickens. But there was nothing she could see at the moment other than the first assumption that the author was talking to another adult, not a child, and that the man had a son.

She stood up and stretched. The sky was getting darker which, in Manchester terms, meant it was going from battleship grey to a deep shade of charcoal. The days were short at this time of the year.

She hadn't eaten yet today, other than a coffee in the morning. She checked inside the fridge; some very good chocolate from Valrhona, a lump of cheese that had seen better days in the Iron Age, half a pint of milk that smelt like it was ready to make cheese, and four bottles of wine.

Not an advert for healthy living.

She promised herself for the second time in two days that she would start to exercise soon. A new gym membership would be her Christmas present to herself.

Jayne realised at that moment that she was becoming a sort of Bridget Jones character, promising to change but not actually committing to it.

At least she didn't smoke. That was not one of her vices. Nor did she keep a diary. Perhaps she would buy herself one for Christmas and really live the cliché.

Mr Smith meowed and she remembered she didn't have any of his gourmet cat food either. She could live on mouldy cheese, but Mr Smith deserved to be fed correctly. She was not going to abandon her duties to him.

She checked the computer screen one more time, looking for a flash of inspiration, but none came. Nor was it ever likely to happen.

She remembered her dad's words. 'You can never solve your problems by staring at a screen, love. Get away from the box, take a walk, a shower, or jump up and down singing *Land of Hope and Glory*, but do something not sit on your bum.'

Robert favoured long walks himself, or at least he used to until the uncertainties of early-onset Alzheimer's made that impossible. Now it was Vera who gave him inspiration.

Jayne put on her coat and decided to walk to the local Tesco Express. As soon as she stepped out of the door and walked to her gate, she realised this might not be such a good idea. A wind from Siberia nearly knocked her down as rain began to sheet across the empty street, soaking everything that got in its way.

Jayne was tempted to turn back and return to the warm and comfort of her kitchen. She stared at her car. Should she drive?

'Pull your big girl's knickers up, Jayne,' she said out loud, 'it's only a five-minute walk. You've seen worse weather on top of Helvellyn.'

Paul and she were avid walkers when they first got married, attacking the Wainwrights and the Derbyshire Dales with gusto. But somehow they had gradually got tired of it and, as with much in their marriage, it petered out until they were doing nothing together any more.

A shame, but she couldn't change the past, just accept it. The past had already been and gone.

She pulled her coat tightly around her neck and strode down to the main road, turning right at the top next to the library. As she hurried past, she glanced across at the noticeboard standing stoutly beside the front door.

Behind the glass were the usual flyers and notices. In one corner, an old poster for the Manchester Literature Festival in October was looking yellow and forlorn. She had actually been to one of the events; a talk on the life and works of Elizabeth Gaskell, who was writing about Manchester at roughly the same time as Dickens' visit to the city.

What was the name of the lecturer? Jayne had chatted to him afterwards. Hadn't he said he specialised in Victorian literature and the North of England? He even organised walks around the city that took in the landmarks popularised by famous authors.

What was his name?

Tom Smithson, that was it.

She stepped into the doorway of the library and began rummaging in the depths of her bag. He had given her his card. It must be here somewhere.

Beneath an old council flyer and two packs of paper tissues, she found it.

She pulled out her mobile phone and rang the number on the off chance he would answer.

He did, after two rings.

'Smithson here.'

She liked the tenor of his voice. It was clipped, almost military in tone. Had he been in the army?

'Hello, Mr Smithson. I don't know if you remember me, my name is Jayne Sinclair. We met after your talk on

Elizabeth Gaskell during the Manchester Literature Festival in October.'

'Of course I remember you, Mrs Sinclair – you were the genealogist, weren't you? A fascinating profession. My own family doesn't go back very far, I'm afraid. Only to the nineteen-thirties.'

Jayne was about to tell him that he was wrong. Of course his family went further back than that, otherwise how could he exist? But she realised this was neither the time nor place.

Instead she said, 'I've come across an interesting case, Mr Smithson, involving Charles Dickens. I wonder if I could pick your brains?'

'That's not a problem, Mrs Sinclair. We could meet in my rooms at the university early next week, I'm at work until the Christmas Eve. The students have all departed to wherever students depart to at this time of the year, so I'm just doing admin right now. And there's enough of that to sink a battleship.'

Jayne sucked in her breath. 'Next week is a bit late, I'm afraid. You see, I have to finish this case at the latest by the end of tomorrow.'

'You are in a hurry. Well, I suppose I could fit you in early tomorrow morning. I have a staff meeting at ten, so how about before that time? Let's meet for a coffee at nine in Christie's Bistro. it's just off Oxford Road close to the University.'

'That'll be perfect, Mr Smithson, thank you for making time for me.'

'Please call me Tom. I'll see you tomorrow, Jayne, at nine.'

The phone clicked off in a very efficient manner. Jayne felt pleased with herself. It may not come to much but at least she might get a few clues to point her in the right direction.

Now it was time to point herself in the direction of the supermarket. She could almost hear Mr Smith whining dog-like for his food.

She stepped out into the gale that was a December afternoon in Manchester and was immediately pushed backwards by the wind.

Time to struggle forward, Jayne. She put her head down and forced herself to walk down the road.

Nothing was going to stop her now. Even the winter in the light and the winter in the shade.

CHAPTER SEVENTEEN

October 4, 1843
Manchester

As they stepped out of the Theatre Royal on to Fountain Street after the play, it was Ainsworth who spoke first. 'What did you think of the company's *Hamlet*, Charles?' he asked cautiously.

'It was… capital,' answered Dickens.

'And the acting?'

'Massive and concrete,' Dickens pronounced.

'No, what did you really think of the performance?'

'I've seen worse Hamlets, but I can't think of any at this moment.'

They both laughed.

'I have to say I agree. To call it terrible would be to offer a compliment.'

On either side of Fountain Street, hawkers had positioned their carts to attack the crowds leaving the theatre. Toffee apples and chestnuts seemed to be particularly popular. But Ainsworth stopped in front of his favourite cart.

Tripe and Trotters.

'I'm feeling a little peckish. Would you like some, Charles?'

Dickens looked across at the delicacies displayed in the light of a flaming Naphtha lamp, which seemed to add a soupçon of flavour to the food. 'I think I'll forgo the pleasure, Ainsworth.'

'You don't know what you are missing.'

He ordered a sheep's trotter. The toothless hawker congratulated him on his choice, selecting a particularly gelatinous trotter and setting it on a fold of newspaper. Ainsworth drizzled vinegar over the sheep's foot through the holes in the cork of a ginger ale bottle.

He held the food up to the light from the lamp. 'I grew up on these. The food of the gods.' He chomped down on the trotter, sucking up the jelly and the vinegar as if it were his last meal on earth. After he had finished sucking every tender, gelatinous morsel, he threw the paper and assorted bones into the gutter, wiping his face with the back of his sleeve. 'You should try it just once, Charles.'

'I think I would rather eat the hind leg of a donkey.'

'I tried that once, it wasn't bad.'

As they walked away, the actor who played Hamlet rushed up to the cart and ordered two trotters.

'Perhaps that explains the quality of the acting,' said Dickens. 'The man was desperate to get off stage to partake of this delicacy.'

'I don't blame him, the rest of the cast were worse than him. The opening was bad and it went rapidly downhill from there.'

Dickens took Ainsworth's arm and hurried them away, frightened the actor might recognise him and ask for a review. 'The King and Queen seated on two armchairs placed on top of a kitchen table lacked a regal touch,' he whispered.

'Why did the King cough throughout the performance? I wonder if he had risen from the grave specially to take the role.'

'I particularly liked the audience participation, turning a tragedy into a comedy with a few chosen words.'

'They certainly enjoyed helping out the Prince. "Whether it is nobler in mind to suffer the slingshots and arrows of outrageous despair" was followed by helpful shouts from the audience of "Yes", "No", and "Let's toss for it". I had to suppress a smile.'

'Poor Hamlet, I thought I knew him well.'

'Wiping his fingers on a white towel after handing back the skull of Yorick was a nice touch, though. Or at least it would have been if somebody in the audience hadn't then shouted "Waiter" in the loudest voice.'

'Perhaps he had eaten the tripe before the performance?'

'And the trotters were dessert.'

They both came to halt, laughing loudly as passers-by stared at them as if they were fools.

'I am sorry, Charles, my city has a long way to go to catch up with the London Theatre.'

'We are spoilt, Ainsworth, by actors of the calibre of Dillon, George Bennett or the late Edward Elton.'

'The ghost was well done, was it not? All shimmering voice and clanking chains, waiting in the wings.'

'But why did he carry the manuscript on the end of a stick, referring to it constantly when he forgot his lines…?'

They both began laughing again as they turned the corner into Market Street.

Dickens spoke though his laughter. 'What was the point of the musical interlude after Hamlet's ghost vanished from the stage?'

'Ah, I'm afraid that's probably a request from the audience. They do like their music and their skits in a play. Since the passing of the new Act, we are seeing many more plays with these interludes.'

'One day they'll drop the play and we will have one long musical interspersed with comedy sketches.'

'That is more than likely.'

'Mr Shakespeare will be turning in his grave.'

'Along with Hamlet and Yorick and the King.'

'And Uncle Tom Cobley, no doubt.'

Ainsworth stopped walking in front of a chophouse. 'Shall we have supper?'

'I think not. Today's efforts have exhausted me. Seeing Fanny was wonderful, seeing her husband less so.'

Piccadilly was quiet. The hawkers had vanished and the shops were shuttered and closed.

'How is your sister?'

'As well as can be expected, but she was never a healthy woman. The move to Manchester was supposed to help, but I wonder whether this is the right atmosphere for her and her son. He is not strong and I fear for his future.'

The dark looming towers of Manchester Royal Infirmary were reflected in the dark pool that languished in the front of the building.

To one side, the lunatic asylum was temporarily quiet, a single lamp burning on the third floor.

A scream rent the air, wailing for a minute before ceasing as suddenly as it had begun.

'The poor inmates. There but for the grace of God go we, Charles,' said Ainsworth. 'Imagine being confined in such a place.'

'If you weren't mad before you went in, you were sure to be mad after spending one night in such a place. All life begins in folly and ends in madness.'

'That sounds particularly depressing.'

Out of the darkness loomed a stout man, his face barely illuminated by a lamp carried on the end of a long stick, giving him the appearance of a pale white ghost.

As he floated closer to them, his body coalesced into something more solid. 'Evenin', gents,' he said in a deep voice.

Dickens visibly relaxed. 'I thought you weren't of this world. A ghost.'

The man chuckled. 'That's what my wife says. But I do meet quite a few ghosts on my walks. I'm the night watchman. After the troubles last year you need to be careful – mark my words, gentlemen.'

'You meet g-ghosts?' stammered Dickens.

'They often keep me company of a night. There's only a few you need watch out for, the rest are friendly enough.' He lifted his battered hat. 'I'd best be on my way. Evenin', gents.'

Dickens and Ainsworth walked on in silence, each in his own world, but each keeping a watchful eye on the shadowed doorways.

Eventually Ainsworth said, 'You really intend to visit Grindley's mill tomorrow?'

'I do.'

'Be prepared for the noise. I recommend waxed paper.'

'Waxed paper?'

'For your ears.' Ainsworth mimed screwing up the paper to form ear plugs.

'And afterwards, a tour of Manchester with a guide provided by Mrs Gaskell.'

They stopped outside the front door of the Adelphi. 'I hope it doesn't make a bad impression on you, Charles. We are a growing city and in our development many mistakes have been made. But there is an energy, a passion here that is missing from other places. It is not for nothing that our symbol is the worker bee.'

'You are still a good salesman for your city, Harrison.'

'Remember, tomorrow we will have the dinner for the speakers at the Athenaeum. I will send a coach to pick you up at seven. Disraeli and Cobden will be there. It won't be a formal affair, but you'll enjoy some most convivial company.'

'I look forward to it.'

Outside the door of the Adelphi, they parted ways with a quick handshake; Ainsworth to his lodgings and Dickens to his rooms.

After having undressed, christened the new chamber pot and washed his face, Dickens relaxed back in his bed.

It had been a good day, if tiring. A day to see his beautiful sister. The magic had gone down well, particularly with young Harry; the days of practising his tricks had paid off.

Tomorrow would be long and equally tiring but he was looking forward to it. A novelist had to experience all that was possible. It was all corn to the mill that was a writer's mind. These were hard times and it was important to understand what was happening.

His experience as a reporter and the trip to the schools of Yorkshire in 1841 had shown him the relevance of understanding the true nature of what was happening around the country.

Perhaps a novel would spring from this visit? At least it had taken his mind off the failure of Chuzzlewit and the failings of his publishers.

He wetted his fingers and extinguished the candle.

Nestling between the linen sheets, he thought again of the theatre and the spectre of Hamlet's ghost. In better hands, the clanking of the chains, the paleness of the white face and the spectral quality of the actor's voice could have created a magical, not comic, effect.

Once again, just before he lost consciousness he heard the floorboards creak and soft steps on the wood.

He closed his eyes even more tightly.

Tonight, he was too tired to be visited by the ghosts of the past.

CHAPTER EIGHTEEN

Tuesday, December 17, 2019
Didsbury, Manchester

With the cat fed, herself bathed and dried after her trip to the supermarket, and dinner cooked and eaten, Jayne felt a lot better. She sat down in front of her computer and checked her messages.

There were the usual marketing emails from Jo Malone, Amazon and other places where she had bought goods in the past. She immediately deleted those without even opening them. There was an invitation from Cheadle Genealogical Society to talk at one of their monthly meetings. She wrote back, politely declining for the foreseeable future due to commitments, but gave them the names of two other genealogists to contact. She loved doing these talks but felt at the moment she couldn't commit to anything, especially as the trip to Australia in February would take her out of the country.

Then she spotted an email from Ronald Welsh.

Dear Mrs Sinclair,

It was wonderful to meet you yesterday.

After your question about where the charity had found the book, I took the trouble of revisiting the shop. Without letting them know about the book's rarity, I discovered they had found the box of books in a house clearance they had performed on an old place in Cheetham Hill.

This immediately aroused my suspicion so I went through the book with a fine-tooth comb and found a tiny book mark embossed on the back inside leaf.

The mark bears the initials JC and the date 1848. I have enclosed a picture of the mark for you with this email.

From my research, it appears to belong to James Crossley, who was an author, bibliophile, literary scholar and book collector. He set up the Chetham Society based at the famous Chetham's Library in 1843, with Thomas Corser, Francis Robert Raines and others. Its purpose was to edit and publish historical works relating to Lancashire and Cheshire. In the following years he personally edited many of its publications, including the autobiographical tracts of John Dee, the magician at the court of Elizabeth I.

He is said to have collected 100,000 books at his residence in Chorlton-on-Medlock and later at Stocks House, Cheetham Hill.

He supplied the novelist William Ainsworth with historical material and ideas, including that author's famous novel on the Pendle Witches.

Unfortunately, there is also a negative aspect to his career. He supposedly perpetrated a literary fraud – the forging of Fragment on Mummies by Sir Thomas Browne. The bogus nature of the Fragment, given by Crossley to Simon Wilkin to publish, is now regarded as highly probable, but Crossley never confessed to it.

He never married and on his death his library was put for auction in 1881.

So that's my latest news, Mrs Sinclair. Given the suspicion of fraud against Mr Crossley, it is even more important that you discover the identity of the man mentioned in the dedication.

I am still convinced the book is genuine, everything tells me that it is. However, if we could discover who the man was, and whether he had any connection to Dickens, it would make the proof incontrovertible.

Thank you for your time and energy.

All the best,

Ronald Welsh
Searcher

That was literally a turn-up for the book.

As Jayne finished reading the email, her mobile phone rang. It was Ronald.

'Hello, Mrs Sinclair, did you get my email?'

'Just reading it now, Ronald. It looks very interesting. This Crossley could be an angle to pursue.' She then detailed her research so far, promising to send an email of the possible suspects she had isolated. Then she explained why it was going to be very difficult to find the man in the time allotted.

'I know it's a difficult task, Mrs Sinclair, that's why we picked you.'

Jayne didn't know what to answer. His faith in her was touching.

'Why don't we meet up tomorrow? I can help you. I'm a good researcher, the best.'

'I don't know, I'm used to working alone.'

'At least let's meet. You can show me your possibles instead of emailing them to me?'

Jayne finally agreed. 'I'll see you outside Central Library at ten thirty.' She could see him after her meeting with Tom Smithson.

'Great, see you tomorrow,' he said enthusiastically before ringing off.

Jayne wasn't looking forward to the meeting. There were just too few clues to help her isolate the correct Robert Duckworth. A sigh of despair welled up in her.

What was wrong? She had never failed in the past, why would she start now?

A little voice in her head whispered: 'There's always a first time, Jayne. Don't think you are better than you are.'

She dismissed the voice immediately. There must be a clue somewhere. She went over her research one more time, looking for inspiration, but none came.

By the time she had finished it was 10.15 p.m.

Where had the time gone?

Mr Smith was standing beside the patio door, ready to go out. At least the wind and the rain had abated, leaving a calm but cold, damp evening.

She stood up and opened the door. He vanished like smoke through the small gap, disappearing into the night.

She yawned and stretched. She had done enough for this evening. Time to get a good night's sleep and hope that she could narrow the field more tomorrow when she went to Central Library.

Before she turned off her computer, she did one last check of her list.

Which one of these men was her Robert Duckworth? In truth, it could be any of them. For the first time, Jayne felt her heart sink.

Time was running out.

How was she going to discover which one it was?

CHAPTER NINETEEN

October 5, 1843
Manchester

The carriage arrived for Dickens exactly on time at 11 a.m.

Customarily, he was punctilious in his choice of wardrobe.

As he was visiting a mill and walking later in the afternoon, he decided on wearing his everyday clothes; loose, large-checked pattern trousers, a brown coat, belt instead of braces, a bright red silk cravat, his yellow waistcoat, a stout walking stick and even stouter boots.

To top off the outfit he settled on his new felt hat, which he set well back on his head, cocked on one side.

After examining himself in the mirror and pronouncing himself fit to face the world, he strode out to the waiting carriage; a handsome four-wheeler with an elegantly matched pair of bays and a liveried footman.

It was certainly far more comfortable than the cabs he had taken the last few days. The interior was lined in silk and upholstered in a plush purple velvet. And when the carriage started forward, even the cobbles seemed less noisy and certainly far less bumpy, almost as if the road had been ironed flat.

'How long to Mr Grindley's mill?' he shouted up at the footman.

'I reckon about five minutes, sir,' an Irish voice explained. 'Sure, we just have to go across Great Ancoats Street and the canal and we're there.'

'I could have walked.'

'But it would not have been as comfortable, sir.' There was a slight pause. 'If his honour would be requiring some refreshment, he'll find a selection in the compartment on his left.'

'Thank you.' Dickens opened the lid and saw decanters of port, whisky, gin and sherry lined in a row, with two shot glasses held in a slot on the lid. Grindley did travel well.

Dickens relaxed back as the carriage and its horses trotted swiftly forward. On either side, the shops of Manchester gradually vanished to be replaced by the dark, forbidding walls of the mills, tall chimneys belching smoke into the crisp air of autumn.

There were not many people on the streets, but through the fogged windows of the mills, Dickens could see shadows moving within. The noise was constant too; a combination of the mechanical, rhythmic pounding of the looms shuttling backwards and forwards, and the constant throb, throb, throb of the steam engines.

The carriage pulled a sharp left beneath a cast-iron entrance. Mr Grindley was standing proudly at the door surrounded by his managers, his fingers perched in his waistcoat pockets and resting on his large stomach.

The coach eased to a stop, the footman jumped down and a door was opened. Dickens stood up and was greeted immediately.

'My good friend, what a pleasure to see you at my humble establishment.'

Dickens felt like royalty descending from on high to greet his subjects. He was escorted through a small unprepossessing entrance, Grindley talking all the time.

'The mill has four buildings at the moment, all producing or finishing the finest cotton cloth. I opened the first, the Waterloo Mill, in 1818. The second followed in 1825, named after the great duke himself.'

'You called it Arthur Wellesley?' said Dickens with a glint in his eye.

'No, sir, we called it the Wellington Mill.'

'Ah, I see.'

'The third we opened in 1834, which we called Talavera, after the duke's famous victory in Spain against the French.'

'I see a theme running through your names, sir. What did you call this building?'

'This one we opened just two years ago, Mr Dickens. It employs the latest engines and the most modern power looms to Mr Roberts' design. I called this one…'

Dickens waited for the name of one of the duke's battles.

'…Grindley's Mill.'

For some reason, Dickens was disappointed. It displayed a certain lack of imagination on the owner's part.

'This mill cost near on twenty-three thousand pounds to build, sir. What do you think of that?'

'It is an uncommonly large amount of money.'

'Indeed it is, sir. Let me escort you around.'

They began walking up the stairs to the first floor.

'How many people work here?'

'At the moment, we employ 876 hands – 232 men, 404 women and 240 children or thereabouts. We can never be certain of the exact number of children.'

'And what ages are the children?'

'I don't employ any of them under ten years old. I believe firmly, sir, unlike other mill owners, that one should never have younger children in a mill despite their undoubted aptitude for the work.'

'Aptitude?'

'The children are small and have dextrous fingertips, sir, perfect for crawling under the machines to twist the broken ends of the cotton threads. This mill has twenty-eight bays, floors of Baltic spruce and six storeys, each of sixteen yards by ninety-two yards. On each floor, the self-acting spinning mules have five hundred spindles.'

Before Dickens could ask another question, Mr Grindley said, 'Here, sir, is one of the wonders of the world.' He pushed open the door and immediately his voice was drowned out by the sound of the mules.

'It is so loud, Mr Grindley,' shouted Dickens.

'You can't spin cotton by being quiet.'

Dickens stared at the hive of activity in front of him. The mules made a clack, clack, clack as they moved backwards and forwards on their cast-iron wheels set in grooves on the pine floor, the spindles spinning rapidly to wind on the lengths of cotton.

In front of the machines, workers – both men and women – attended to the spindles, moving quickly from one to the other, repairing breakages and ensuring the shuttles were running freely. Beneath the mules, Dickens could see the small figures of children crawling between the moving machinery, the fingers reaching up and darting down to avoid being caught by the moving metal arms.

The air was damp and humid, thick with motes and fibres of cotton dust floating like a thin mist above the machines.

He bent close to Mr Grindley's face and shouted in his ear, 'Why is it so hot?'

'To prevent the cotton drying and breaking. Cotton loves damp and warmth. Even in the middle of winter, we keep our mill nice and cosy.'

One or two of the workers glanced up at Dickens quickly before returning back to the shuttles and their cotton.

'How long do people work here, Mr Grindley?'

'Only twelve hours a day, Mr Dickens. I don't believe people should work longer than that. Plus they have every Sunday off for church and the like.'

Dickens coughed twice, finding the fibres irritating his throat. A worker in front of him raised her hand and, almost mechanically, another took her place as she left the mule.

'Time for a water break. The cotton dries the throat, Mr Dickens. And talking of dry throats, would you like to partake of some luncheon? I have rather a pleasant wine I'd like you to try.'

'That would be most agreeable, Mr Grindley.'

The mill owner took him by the arm and led him from the floor. Dickens took one last look over his shoulder at the never-ceasing movement of the machines and the people manning them.

Nobody looked back at him.

CHAPTER TWENTY

Wednesday, December 18, 2019
Christie's Bistro, Manchester

Jayne Sinclair turned up early at Christie's Bistro to find Tom Smithson already waiting for her.

The contrast between this meeting and her last at Mackie Mayor couldn't have been more obvious. Here she was surrounded by books, stained-glass windows, high ceilings and portraits of old professors of the university.

'Have you ever been here before, Mrs Sinclair?'

Jayne did a 360-degree turn to take in the place. 'No, I haven't. It's impressive, isn't it?'

'It's the old Science Library, now repurposed as a café and restaurant. I remember it when it was a quiet place to escape and read. Now it's packed during term-time but, as you see,' he pointed to the empty tables, 'it's a little bit too early for most students. Can I get you a coffee?'

'No, please, it's my treat as I am picking your brains this morning.'

'I'll have another latte then. My brain needs more of a kickstart than it used to when I was young and I find caffeine to be the one drug that works effectively.'

'I know the feeling.'

After ordering lattes for both of them, Jayne returned to the comfortable armchairs and sat down.

'How can I help you, Mrs Sinclair? I'm afraid I must be so direct as I have to leave in an hour for one of those interminable staff meetings to discuss the cleaning arrangements of the staff toilets. The bane of any lecturer's life, I'm afraid.'

'No problem, Mr Smithson. I'd like you to tell me as much as you can about Charles Dickens and his relationship with Manchester.'

The old don nodded his head. 'Before I answer your question, may I ask why you are so interested in this particular topic? I thought you said you were a genealogical researcher?'

'I am, but I've been asked to find the family of a Robert Duckworth who lived in the city in the 1840s.' Jayne continued to explain the request from Michael Underwood and Ronald Welsh, showing Smithson the photocopies of the book.

'Fascinating. This would be a discovery of immense proportions in the world of Dickens scholarship. Firstly, an unknown first edition, and secondly, a link to the city and Dickens' visit here in October 1843.'

'He did come here?'

'Oh, definitely. The speech at the fundraising event in support of the Athenaeum was reported in all the major newspapers, including the *Manchester Guardian*.'

'So there is a possibility that the dedication on this book is important?'

'More than important. Vital for understanding Dickens and his work, particularly his most popular novella, *A Christmas Carol*.'

'Did he come to Manchester often?'

'Many times, both to give readings, open libraries and to visit his sister and her children until her death in 1848. It is believed her child, Harry, was the inspiration for Tiny Tim in the book, but I have my doubts.'

'Why?'

'Harry was described as weak and sickly. Tiny Tim is far more handicapped, needing to be carried everywhere by his father, Bob Cratchit. At the end of the novella, Dickens portrays a happy future for Tiny Tim under the benevolent watch of Scrooge. In truth, Harry died six years later in January 1849. Even worse, Dickens' beloved sister, Fanny, had died three months earlier.'

'A sad story.'

'Her husband, Henry Burnett, stayed in Manchester for at least ten years afterwards, marrying a woman from Bury in 1859.'

'Dickens came back to see him?'

'Probably not. He disapproved of his sister's husband. The man's religion meant that he had given up a career in the opera and forced Fanny to do the same. But Dickens had many friends in the city. Harrison Ainsworth, the novelist who wrote *Rookwood* and *Jack Sheppard*, was close for a time until they drifted apart. Dickens even met his mistress, Ellen Ternan, here when they both acted in a drama at the Free Trade Hall called *The Frozen Deep*. He eventually left his wife for this woman. The relationship was kept very quiet, though, for fear of offending Victorian morals and sensibility. You have to understand that Dickens was the rock star of his day, the most famous author in the world. Equivalent to a Mick Jagger or a George Michael.'

'Or a David Bowie?'

'Yes, he would be a better example.'

'Does the name James Crossley ring any bells for you?'

'Coming from Manchester, how could he not? He was the foremost collector of books in the city.'

'Yesterday, one of my clients discovered an embossed symbol and a date in the book. It was 1848.'

'Interesting, the date of Dickens' sister's death. A link, perhaps? Come to think of it, Crossley found the Chetham Society in 1843, the same year Dickens visited Manchester.'

'Chetham Society?'

'Really, Mrs Sinclair, you live in Manchester and you have never been to Chetham's Library?'

Jayne shook her head. 'Actually, it's Ms Sinclair and I haven't.'

'The Portico Library? The Athenaeum? The Friends Meeting House? The Hidden Church?'

Jayne shook her head at all four.

'It's very Manchester to ignore the beauty of the city. You should come on one of my tours, where I explain the significance of all these places. You see, when Dickens visited Manchester it was the centre of the world's cotton trade, the shock city of the Industrial Revolution. People came from all over the world to study the city;

most were appalled at the conditions of the workers, but amazed at their productivity and industry. Engels wrote his *The Condition of the Working Class in England* while living in the city and published it in 1844, the year after Dickens visited to open the Athenaeum. De Tocqueville, Tain and even Otto von Bismarck also came to marvel at the city's excellence at manufacturing and moralise at the depths of its poverty.'

'You said he gave a speech at a soiree to raise funds for the Athenaeum?'

'You can still see the building, it's part of Manchester Art Gallery now. I think most people expected the standard address – happy to be here, a fine building, a worthy cause. You know the sort of thing. But Dickens used the occasion to lambast the mill owners, bankers and worthies assembled before him, telling them to do more to educate people and improve society.'

'I bet that went down well.'

'Like a slap around the face with a dead mackerel. But ten days later, he started writing *A Christmas Carol* and expounded on those very themes. Nowadays, nobody remembers the mill owners but everybody knows the story of Ebenezer Scrooge and Tiny Tim. The enduring power of art over commerce, I think. But I would say that, I'm a lecturer.'

He glanced at the large clock on the wall.

Jayne quickly asked him another question. 'Have you ever heard of Robert Duckworth?'

Tom Smithson shook his head slowly. 'I do not recall the name ever coming up in my research. But reading the dedication, it is obvious that he and Dickens had a close friendship. As far as I remember, Dickens did send out signed editions of *A Christmas Carol,* but only to his closest business or personal acquaintances. He was very proud of this book and wanted to share it.'

The lecturer sat forward in his armchair and gathered his books.

'Does any of these date or addresses seem familiar perhaps?' She put the list of Robert Duckworths on the table she had discovered in the census. Smithson picked it up and read intently.

'As I said, I've never come across a Robert Duckworth in my research. And looking at their occupations, these people are all mill workers. Dickens enjoyed the company of many people from different walks of life, but cotton piecers were not generally part of his normal milieu in Manchester.'

He handed the paper back to Jayne and stood up.

She thought quickly. 'One last question, Mr Smithson – if you wanted to discover Robert Duckworth, where would you go?'

Smithson stared into mid-air and then pointed to the bookcase behind Jayne. 'Given that James Crossley once owned this book, I would go to a library.'

'Which one?'

'The one he was most closely connected to. Chetham's.'

'It's still in Manchester?'

'And has been since 1653. You might find your missing Robert Duckworth there.'

'Thank you for your time, Mr Smithson.' She reached into her wallet. 'If you think of anything else, please don't hesitate to call me, Mr Smithson.'

He accepted the card and picked up his books, taking a few steps towards the door, before turning back. 'You might also want to check out the John Rylands Library. Dickens and another Manchester writer, Elizabeth Gaskell, were close. He published her first short story and serialised her novels *North and South* and *Cranford* in his *Household Words* magazine. There are quite a few letters in the library from him to her.'

'Thanks, I'll bear it in mind. I still want to go to Central Library and check out the rate books and the parish registers.'

He turned to go and then turned back once more. 'You know, I would love to see the book.'

'It's being auctioned tomorrow, but I can ask my clients if they could let you see it before it leaves the country.'

'It's going to America?'

'They believe an American library will buy it.'

He shook his head. 'Shame. What a shame.'

CHAPTER TWENTY-ONE

October 5, 1843
Manchester

Dickens was feeling rather full as he waited outside the cast-iron gates of Grindley's mill, even though he had eaten little of the vast array of dishes on offer.

Northern mill owners were proud of keeping a good table for lunch. Tongues in aspic, cold collations, a selection of fowl, roasted and boiled vegetables, desserts, cakes, trifles, puddings and nutty Cheshire cheeses, all accompanied by excellent Rieslings and fine ports.

The company had been fascinating; Silas Grindley was obviously proud of the factory and its productivity. His managers were quiet in his company, only speaking when asked a direct question.

'And what do you do, Mr Fotheringill?'

'He makes me money is what he does, Mr Dickens,' interrupted Grindley. 'Fotheringill here is the best maintenance engineer of steam engines in the city. My engines are always working, never a day off for steam, hey, Fotheringill?'

'No, sir, Mr Grindley. Mr Roberts and Mr Fairbairn builds a fine engine. As long as you look after her, she will look after you.'

'You use the feminine pronoun, Mr Fotheringill?' asked Dickens.

For the first time the man looked animated. 'Indeed I do, Mr Dickens.'

'The steam engines are as temperamental as women and twice as expensive to run,' said Grindley. 'But in Fotheringill's good hands they become as docile as whipped dogs.'

'Thank you, Mr Grindley. I will remember that for the future.'

Dickens checked his gold hunter. The man, this Mr Duckworth, was late. Dickens felt decidedly uncomfortable standing outside the factory gates, everybody staring at him as they walked by.

Where was he??

Just as Dickens was about to turn and re-enter the mill, a man ran up and shouted, 'Mr Dickens, Mr Dickens.' He was slight and small, but with a pleasing freshness and innocence, not more than twenty-five years old, Dickens guessed.

'Sorry I'm late, sir. It took me longer than I expected.'

The man was slightly out of breath and the voice was northern, that mixture of vowel sounds resembling brass and muck.

'Are you Mr Duckworth?' Dickens asked.

'I am, sir.' A woman joined him, panting too.

'Sent by Mrs Gaskell to guide me around Manchester?'

'Again correct, sir. And this is Miss Lizzie Burns.'

The woman nodded her head.

'And you are to guide me too?'

'I am, surr.' This voice was decidedly Irish. She was dressed in the shawls and long skirts common for the workers in the mills, but there was none of the deference usually displayed by the factory hands about this woman. She looked him straight in the eye with her head held high rather than staring down at her feet. 'And what does Mr Dickens want to see?'

'Everything. The good, the bad and the phenomenally ugly.'

'There is plenty of the last in Manchester,' said Lizzie Burns.

'Lizzie knows areas of Manchester where even I would not dare to go, Mr Dickens,' added Robert Duckworth.

'Lead on, MacDuff.'

They began to walk down the road away from the mill. 'It's "lay on", Mr Dickens.'

'Pardon?'

'The quote from Macbeth. It's "lay on, MacDuff".'

'You have read your Shakespeare, Mr Duckworth?'

'I have, sir,' said the man, proudly. 'All except the later plays. But I'm working my way round to them when I have the time.'

'And when you don't?'

'I work to support my family, sir.'

'Your profession?'

'A clerk, sir. To an ancient firm of solicitors, Voles and Harmison.'

'Yet you have time to guide me today?'

'I have recently been dismissed, Mr Dickens.'

Dickens frowned. 'Dismissed? What for?'

'I had the temerity to request a day off at Christmas.'

'And you were dismissed from your post?'

'Precisely, sir. Mr Voles was most adamant that Christmas Day was one of the normal working days of the year.'

'How will you survive?'

'I will get by. Something will turn up. The good Lord will provide.'

Dickens glanced across at Lizzie Burns. 'You have a wife and children?'

Robert Duckworth saw the look and answered immediately. 'I do, sir. A wife and two children. Lizzie here is a friend from the Hall of Science.'

'Hall of Science?'

'A place where working men and women can meet and talk and read and discuss the issues of the day.'

'I would like to see such a place.'

'We were planning on showing you it today,' said Lizzie over her shoulder.

They reached a crossroads. Duckworth stopped and pointed left. 'That way is to Piccadilly, the hospital and your hotel. Straight on is Angel Meadow and the River Irk.'

'What do you suggest, Mr Duckworth?'

'If you want to see how people really liven Manchester, I would go straight on.' Lizzie issued the challenge to Dickens.

'I see no point in returning from whence I came. Not yet, anyway. Lay on, Mr Duckworth and Miss Burns.'

'You might not like what you see, Mr Dickens, being a gentleman and all that.'

Again, the memories of shoe-blacking in London flashed through his mind. If only they knew what he had been through. 'I have seen a lot in London, Miss Burns.'

'You haven't seen Angel Meadow.'

They carried on walking, Lizzie Burns leading the way.

Across the street a sweep was pushing his cart followed by two coal-blackened boys, one of whom was eating a sooty piece of bread with relish.

'Weep, Weee-eeeep for hire. Weeeeeppppp,' he shouted as the other boy banged a sooty drum, staring at the pedestrians, their white eyes and teeth a stark contrast to their soot-blackened faces.

On the road next to them carts hurried past, laden with bales of cotton or rolls of finished goods, the rattle of their metalled wheels a sharp contrast to the deep throb of the steam engines and the clatter of the looms in the mills lining the road.

Dickens looked around, taking it all in, making mental notes of all the sights and sounds; the streets of Manchester his own magic lantern showing him image after image.

Lizzie turned a corner. 'Angel Street is this way. Most of the people here are Irish. Some from Mayo and

Roscommon, others from Tipperary. There's even a few spalpeens from Cork, but we avoid those tinkers.'

In the blink of an eye, the area had changed. On the main roads, the gutters were relatively clean and the streets cobbled. But just a few steps away, they became little more than compacted earth with a trench on either side, filled with foul-smelling mud.

A child was standing barefoot in one of those trenches, prodding some rotting rubbish with a stick.

Lizzie Burns was watching him. 'It gets worse the further you go inside.'

Dickens pointed to the long row of terraced houses, divided every fifty yards by a narrow, dark alley leading to an even darker interior. 'Who owns these places?'

'Most are built and rented by the mill owners. The people who do the work have to live somewhere.'

'Others are built by speculators who know they have a ready market.'

'How many people live here?'

'Let's go and look, shall we?' Lizzie again threw out her challenge.

Dickens followed her towards one of the alleys. At its entrance, a young man was leaning against the wall smoking a pipe.

'Don't see you much these days, Lizzie.'

'I don't come much, Micky.'

'Who's the toff?' The man jerked his saliva-sodden pipe stem towards Dickens.

'Nobody. A friend.'

The man looked at Dickens from tip to toe. 'I like his keks.'

'There's to be no trouble, Micky, understand?'

The man nodded, slotting his pipe back into a gap between his teeth. 'No trouble, Lizzie, just sayin'.'

Lizzie sniffed and walked on, followed by Dickens and Robert Duckworth. Dickens felt the man's eyes on him all the time.

They entered a long, dark alley with damp drenched brick walls stretching high above their heads. At the end, they came out into a dank, dirty courtyard, surrounded on all four sides by soot-encrusted walls. Stairs led up to the entrance of each tenement where, instead of a door, a filthy sheet of oilskin was hung to block out the weather and the light.

'Each room is occupied by one family. The unlucky ones live in the cellars.'

'Why are they unlucky?' asked Dickens.

'Because of that place.' She pointed off to the left. As Dickens turned his head, his nose became aware of the foulest smell he had ever encountered. Far worse than anything he had ever seen or smelt in any of the rookeries of London.

Once again, his mind drifted off to his youth in London. Why were these memories intruding more and more these days? Had the prospect of bankruptcy brought them back into his mind? Living in Bayham Street, in a similar courtyard, unable to afford school, his father in the debtors prison in Marshalsea, the family split up and divided.

A squalid memory of an even more squalid time.

'There's just one jacks for about a hundred families. When it rains, the sewers overflow and the stuff flows into the cellars.'

'Why would they live there?'

'Where else *can* they live?

Three unloved and uncared-for small children approached them, each barefoot, wearing only the flimsiest of cotton clothes despite the bracing winds of autumn.

'Is there no school?'

'There's talk of a Ragged School opening in Charter Street, but the mill owners aren't too keen. They see learning as a dangerous thing. You don't need to be able to read and write to work beneath a loom.'

Lizzie glanced behind her, hearing a loud noise. It was a rat being cornered by a child.

'We should go now, before the people start to become nervous.'

A few men had come out of one property and were standing at the entrance to the house.

Lizzie took Dickens' arm and led him back the way they had come. Just before they re-entered the dark hole of the alleyway, Dickens looked back.

The child had trapped the rat in an old tin bucket and was banging on top of the lid, gleefully calling to a small grey dog: 'A big 'un, Tommy, for ye!'

They entered the dark tunnel.

Dickens felt like he was leaving hell.

CHAPTER TWENTY-TWO

Wednesday, December 18, 2019
Central Library, Manchester

Jayne hurried down Oxford Road towards Central Library. She had decided to leave her car where it was. Better that than spend an hour navigating the one-way system and another forty years looking for a parking space.

Luckily, it was one of those beautiful days that occasionally disturbed a great drab Manchester winter. The sky was a wonderful eggshell blue with just a few aircraft contrails like strokes of paint across it. Even the air was fresh, with just a chill in the nose to remind her it was still winter.

She was conscious this was her last full day of research. She hadn't got very far, merely isolating the possibilities down to a few suspects.

The whole process reminded her of being a police detective. When investigating any serious crime, the job was to trace suspects, then investigate and eliminate them if possible. In a genealogical investigation the same parameters applied, except the job was to research possible ancestors, look into the past and either eliminate them or confirm a link.

In this case, she had not eliminated enough Robert Duckworths yet. She knew she would be able to discover the truth eventually, but time was not on her side. She had till tonight to report her findings to Michael Underwood.

Ronald was waiting for her outside the doors of Central Library. 'Morning, Mrs Sinclair.' He sounded bright and breezy, almost happy to see her. 'How did your meeting go?'

'Good, let's go inside and I'll brief you.'

As soon as they entered the building, Ronald's mood changed.

He seemed to shrink back into himself, watching the users of the busy library with suspicion, staring at the people's feet as they climbed the stairs to the reading room, listening to the sound of their steps echoing off the walls.

Before they entered the local studies area, Jayne told him everything she had discovered from her meeting with Tom Smithson. 'It wasn't terribly useful at eliminating possibilities, but it did help with the background of Dickens and Manchester.'

'I told you he'd been here often, didn't I?'

'You did, and Mr Smithson confirmed the importance of Manchester to *A Christmas Carol*. He'd like to see the book before it's sold, if that's possible.' She could almost see Ronald shrinking into his coat, becoming more and more uncomfortable.

'You'll have to ask Michael, nothing to do with me.' He glanced around nervously. 'What's the plan here?'

'I want to check out the Manchester rate books. The Census only gives us the details from every ten years, and, in our case, the 1851 Census for Manchester was damaged, only leaving us the 1841 Census complete. However, the Manchester rate books go all the way back to 1706 and are a record of all local property tax-payers in the city. They are a useful substitute for the Census, particularly as they were collected on a yearly basis. They can also help find other Robert Duckworths who may have moved to the city after the Census of 1841.'

'Sounds good.'

'But there is a problem. Unlike the Census, there no other details of age, occupation or family members living in the house – just the tenant, the address and the rateable value of the property.'

Ronald perked up again. 'Brilliant. I love research, you don't have to deal with people.'

'Mr Welsh, please understand I mean no disrespect, but I like to do my research alone. It's my way of making sure I don't miss anything, however insignificant.'

'I understand, Mrs Sinclair. However, with no disrespect, we only have today left. Normally, I would say it is your job to research Robert Duckworth, but given the lack of time, don't you think you could do with some help?'

It was one of Jayne's character flaws; she never asked for help, believing it was up to her to do everything herself. Even when she was a copper, her reports had been scathing. 'PC 4856 needs to understand that asking for help or information is not a weakness, it will encourage her to perform her duties satisfactorily.' It was an almost constant refrain from virtually every assessment from her superiors.

'I can be another pair of eyes, Mrs Sinclair. We don't have a lot of time and I'm used to research.'

Jayne didn't want to argue. Ronald was right. They didn't have enough time and there was a lot of detailed work to be done in the records.

She shrugged her shoulders. 'Okay, Ronald, you can help me – but you need to follow my instructions to the letter, understand?'

'Understood.' He glanced over his shoulder as somebody walked past him. 'Shall we get started?'

They entered the local studies archive and approached the desk. Jayne asked the librarian for the Manchester rate books for 1837 to 1845. It was a wide range, but she thought she should cover as wide a timescale as possible. And with Ronald to help, she should be able to do it quickly.

'We have rate books for those years,' replied the librarian. 'Some of the earlier ones, like 1830, have been lost, though. Let me show you where the microfilms are kept.'

She took them to the cabinet, choosing the correct years. 'You know how to use the reader?'

'Is the Pope a catholic?' answered Ronald.

The librarian cocked her head and frowned.

Jayne quickly spoke. 'We know how to work the machines, thank you.'

'Is there anything else?'

'Possibly the parish and electoral registers later?'

'Just give me a shout when you need them.'

The librarian walked away, checking out Ronald, who was oblivious to her stares.

'Right, Ronald. I'll take 1841 to 1845, you take the early years. These are the Robert Duckworth addresses you are looking for, plus their parishes or areas.'

She showed him her printed list of the ten possible candidates, explaining that the names with red crosses against them were missing from the incomplete 1851 Census and the three names at the bottom were added to it, but missing from 1841 Census.

Ronald stared at it a long time, before saying. 'I understand, it's perfectly clear Mrs Sinclair.

Birth	Address	Family	Job	Residence

1801	Minshull St	Mary, 5 children	Twister	St James Ward XXX
1806	Rogers Rd	Eliza, 4 children	Calico Printer	Angel Meadow
1807	????	Mary, 2 children	Tailor	College Ward XXX
1811	Minehead St	Sarah, 2 children	Cotton Weaver	Ancoats
1816	Howard Lane	Sarah, no children	Power Loom Operator	Stockp't XXX
1816	Ardwick Green	Helen, 5 children	Block Printer	Ardwick
1819	Newberry St	Mary, 2 children	Clerk	St Annes
1817	Halson St	Mary, 4 children	Editor	Chorlton-on-M
1826	Plymouth Grove	Eliza, 3 children	Fustian Shearer	Ardwick
1826	Hanging Ditch	Emily, 2 children	Clerk	Deansgate

Luckily, two microfilm viewers next to each other were free. 'Do you know how to use the machines?' the Librarian asked Ronald.

'Is the Pope—'

Jayne held her hand up to stop him from talking. 'I get the message. Remember, it's a process of elimination. We're looking to see if people appeared on the 1841 Census and on the rate books up to 1844. If they are on the Census but not in the rate books then we can eliminate them.'

'Why?'

'It means they either died or moved away from Manchester before the end of 1843. We will be able to confirm that with the Births, Marriages and Deaths lists. Or they moved to live in Manchester after 1843 and were enumerated on the 1851 Census.'

'Okay, got it.' Ronald took the first microfilm for 1837 out of it's box and threaded it expertly through the machine reader. Staring at the illuminated screen, he began looking for the correct districts.

His concentration on the task was total. Jayne could see that he was totally in his element; the world of documents and words.

She sat down and took out the microfilm for 1841 and checked the areas on her list.

Two hours later and they had finished with all the documents.

Ronald's work on the early years confirmed that all the names on the 1841 Census also appeared in the rate books. However, three names didn't appear on the rate books after 1843. Jayne removed them from her list. One new name appeared on the rate book for 1843, and this name was also on the 1851 Census.

The two other Duckworths in the 1851 Census were not in the rate books before 1845, so Jayne eliminated them. The new list was shortened, but not by much.

Birth	Address	Family	Job	Residence
1806	Rogers Rd	Eliza, 4 children	Calico Printer	Angel Meadow
1811	Minehead St	Sarah, 2 children	Cotton Weaver	Ancoats
1816	Ardwick Green	Helen, 5 children	Block Printer	Ardwick

1819	New-berry St	Mary, 2 children	Clerk	St Annes
1817	Halson St	Mary, 4 children	Editor	Chorlton-on-M

Ronald checked out the list. 'So our Robert Duckworth is one of these people?'

Jayne nodded. 'Probably, unless we have missed somebody. The last person's job is interesting. What sort of editor was he? Could he have known Charles Dickens through his work?'

'It's possible. How do we narrow it down even further?'

Jayne looked at her watch. 'We go over there and get something to eat and another coffee.' She pointed to the café in the corner. 'I don't know about you, but research always makes me hungry for some reason.'

Ronald looked anxious. 'I prefer to stay here, too many people.'

Jayne touched his arm. 'We'll sit in the corner away from people. We need to take a break. Unless I eat now, I'm going to chew your arm off soon.'

Ronald smiled and held up his hand. 'One finger or two?'

CHAPTER TWENTY-THREE

October 5, 1843
Manchester

They hurried towards the right, heading past a graveyard and down some moss-covered steps. Dickens' feet nearly went from under him on the slippery surface but he was quickly grabbed and supported by the strong arms of Lizzie Burns.

'You shouldn't fall over round here, love, you never know what's lying beneath you.'

Dickens descended more cautiously from then on, making sure he watched exactly where he put his feet.

At the bottom of the steps, they came to a bridge over a body of water.

'Dulcie Bridge over the Irk,' said Robert Duckworth. 'Yonder lies Strangeways. You can see the buildings of the workhouse through the smoke. Not a place anyone aspires to, Mr Dickens.'

'People prefer living with the devils in Angel Meadow rather than spend a minute in there?'

'In front of it is the new station to Liverpool. I believe you travelled from London by train, Mr Dickens?'

'I did.'

'And it only took nine hours?'

'That is true. The speed is remarkable. They are talking of a new engine which will reduce the time even further.'

Robert shook his head. 'One day I would love to travel by train.'

'But until hell freezes over, it's Shanks's pony for the likes of us.'

'Shanks's pony?'

'Lizzie means we generally walk everywhere. I took the Omnibus once, but standing on the ledge outside, of course. They were after asking sixpence for a seat. Daylight robbery.'

Robert pointed back across the river. 'To the left are the rookeries of Salford. Slightly better than Manchester—'

'But not much,' interrupted Lizzie. 'At least the air is cleaner.'

Dickens edged over the parapet. Fifty feet below, the river flowed sluggishly like liquid mud. A coal-black, foul-smelling stream with a rainbow film of oil and decay. On the banks, dark, derelict-looking mills with tall chimney stacks belching smoke stood interspersed with shed-like pig sties. Dickens could hear the squeals of the beasts as they luxuriated in the revolting slime and mud. Next to the pigs, two young boys were diving into the desolate waters and surfacing moments later, grasping a metal pipe in their hands.

A foul stench arose from a bubble of gas that had somehow broken through the sludge that had once been a river. Dickens jerked his head back.

Robert Duckworth pointed to each chimney. 'Over there is a tannery. Those two are dyeing factories. You can tell the colour they are using on any particular day by the hue of the river.' He moved quicker now. 'A brewery, tripe works, another dyer's, a foundry, a fustian mill, a calico printers. All their waste and effluent flows into this river.'

'You forgot the waste of forty thousand people. Where else can it go but down there?'

One of the young boys saw them watching from the bridge and waved.

Dickens waved back half-heartedly. 'Why do people live like this, Mr Duckworth?'

Lizzie Burns answered for him. 'How else would they live?'

Dickens nodded once. 'I think I have seen enough.'

'Good, let us repair to one of my favourite places in Manchester. A relic of the past, but one I am sure you will enjoy, Mr Dickens.'

CHAPTER TWENTY-FOUR

October 5, 1843
Manchester

They retraced their steps slightly before turning left and ascending a slight hill past a planless, knotted chaos of houses.

'Where are we going, Robert?'

'To see my friend, Mr Jones. Hopefully Mr Crossley will be there too. They are both extremely excited to meet you.'

Suddenly, the dark, satanic walls of the mills vanished and Dickens was in another world. The buildings were constructed from sandstone and were low to the ground, possessing a singular elegance missing from the rest of Manchester's architecture.

'This is Chetham's, Mr Dickens. Founded in 1653 and still going strong. The college is on the right, but we are going to the library.'

They passed a gatehouse and went through a cobbled yard. The stone buildings were obviously medieval in style.

'Here we are,' announced Robert Duckworth.

Lizzie Burns was hanging back. 'You go ahead. I'll wait here. My sex is not permitted to enter, for fear we'll damage the books with our feminine spells. Or be somehow infected with the desire to learn. Neither is a prospect the library desires.'

Dickens hesitated for a second before he was pushed forward by Duckworth.

Inside the wood was dark and there was that peculiar smell of old books; a combination of mould, dust and learning.

They clattered up some old steps and were met at the top by an ancient librarian, his skin and beard so white he was almost albino. It was as if the man had not seen the light of day for decades. Next to him stood a much smaller but more energetic man, whose whole demeanour radiated enthusiasm.

'May I present Mr Jones, the venerable librarian of Chetham's, and the head of the society, Mr James Crossley.'

The old librarian mumbled a welcome while Crossley leapt forward to grab Dickens' hand. 'A pleasure to finally meet you, sir.'

Dickens shook his hand firmly.

In front of him, shelf after shelf of books rose to a barn-like ceiling. Each bookcase was barred and locked. Inside, Dickens could just make out ancient tomes bound in vellum, their titles etched in gold leaf.

'It is a beautiful library, sir. I did not know the like existed in Manchester.'

'It suffices,' muttered the old librarian.

'We too are proud of our ancient library. Some volumes date back to the sixteenth century.'

'Almost as old as you, Mr Jones,' Robert Duckworth said light-heartedly.

The librarian cupped his ear. 'What? What was that?'

James Crossley held out his arm. 'Come this way into the Reading Room, Dickens.'

The room was wood panelled and quiet. A coat of arms hung over a marble fireplace. On the round table in front, two scholars were examining an old book together, their heads close. In the window alcove, a single man was writing, checking some figures from a book.

Crossley leant in, seeing where Dickens was looking. 'A strange man. German, I think, from the Rhineland. Always borrowing books on political economy, family owns a mill in Salford. Now if you'd care to sign our visitors book, Mr Dickens, I would be obliged to you.'

An open book lay on the desk next to the two scholars. Dickens took the proffered pen, writing the date in letters and signing his name with the usual flourish of curlicues at the bottom.

Dickens then passed the pen to Robert Duckworth, who signed his name in a beautiful script below that of Dickens.

Mr Jones sniffed twice, eyeing Robert suspiciously. He brought the book up close to his face, blowing on the ink to ensure it dried.

'Capital, Mr Dickens. Can I treat you to a glass or three of Madeira?' said Crossley.

Dickens checked the time on the large grandfather clock in the corner. 'I think not, Mr Crossley. I have to deliver my lecture at eight this evening and I would like time to revisit it beforehand.'

They shook hands. 'Thank you for your time, and if you require anything in the future, please let me know.'

'I will, without hesitation.' Dickens turned to his young companion. 'We should leave before Miss Burns abandons us.'

'Of course, Mr Dickens.'

He stood for a moment in the library, gazing at the long rows of books, each in the locked and barred cabinets. 'Such a wonderful place. Remind me to send you some of my books,' he said to Crossley.

'We would be honoured, wouldn't we, Mr Jones?'

'Naturally, all books are welcome,' sniffed Mr Jones again, 'even those from popular authors.'

From the sound of Mr Jones's voice, it seemed popular was not a compliment.

CHAPTER TWENTY-FIVE

October 5, 1843
Manchester

They rejoined Lizzie outside. She had been sitting on a bench at the front door, waiting for them impatiently. 'About time, I thought you'd got lost in there.'

'Nearly,' admitted Dickens. 'I fear time has no meaning in Chetham's. Where to next, Mr Duckworth?'

'I thought you wanted to return to your hotel, Mr Dickens?'

'I do, but not now. It was necessary to tell a little white lie to escape. Much as I adore libraries, I fear being trapped in one is something Dantesque, a version of hell. One needs always to get out and about, to see the world as if it were a magic lantern. In a library, one only sees the world through the eyes of others, not oneself.'

'But education is important, is it not, Mr Dickens?'

'It is key, Mr Duckworth, but it has to be part of our world, not separate from it.'

They walked on past the cathedral and into Deansgate. The area had changed once again, now becoming more elegant and mercantile. Large warehouses, banks, shops, law offices and showrooms abounded.

'This is Manchester's centre of commerce, Mr Dickens.'

'Grindley told me about it. The place where money is made.'

'It is,' said Lizzie, walking in front of the two men, 'and another place so full of charlatans, rogues, vagabonds and thieves could not be imagined.'

'It is not the making of money that is evil, Miss Burns, but the lack of sharing of it. Want and ignorance are the true evil, not those who make money.'

'You should write a book on that theme, Mr Dickens,' she replied.

'I should, shouldn't I?' said Dickens under his breath.

CHAPTER TWENTY-SIX

Wednesday, December 18, 2019
Central Library, Manchester

Jayne ordered a latte and a cheese and ham sandwich for herself. Ronald had tap water.

'You're sure you don't want to eat?'

'Positive. I don't like eating outside, I prefer to cook for myself.'

'You cook at home?'

'Always. Tomato soup. I'm very good at cooking tomato soup. And two slices of bread. I always make sure I have bread. The grains, you know.'

Jayne looked at him. 'You only eat tomato soup? Doesn't it get boring?'

He stared back, not really understanding the question. 'No, I really like it.'

They sat at the back of the café with their backs to the wall. After a minute or so, Ronald appeared to relax, asking, 'What are we going to do next?'

Between mouthfuls of sandwich, Jayne mumbled, 'Good question.' She sipped her coffee, washing down the last of the food. She pulled out her laptop and showed him the list, 'Here are the five contenders we have at the moment.'

Birth	Address	Family	Job	Residence
1806	Rogers Rd	Eliza, 4 children	Calico Printer	Angel Meadow
1811	Mine-head St	Sarah, 2 children	Cotton Weaver	Ancoats
1816	Ardwick Green	Helen, 5 children	Block Printer	Ardwick
1819	New-berry St	Mary, 2 children	Clerk	St Annes
1817	Halson St	Mary, 4 children	Editor	Chorlton-on-M

She scratched her head. 'It could be any of these people.'

'How do we narrow it down further?'

Jayne thought for a long time. 'We've basically exhausted all the relevant Manchester documents. We could check out the parish records for these people, but that would only give us more information about them. What we really need is to discover a link between one of them and Charles Dickens. And particularly his visit to Manchester in October 1843.'

'How do we do that?'

Ronald was relentless in his questioning. Jayne wracked her brain for an answer. She looked out over the library, focusing on the signs for the local studies department. Had she missed anything? Was there a resource that she had forgotten about? The librarian was still behind her desk, moving between her computer and a stack of files.

She drained the last of her coffee and stood up. 'Come on, Ronald.'

'Where are we going?'

'When in doubt, talk to an expert.'

CHAPTER TWENTY-SEVEN

October 5, 1843
Manchester

They strode down Deansgate, past the butchers with its feast of carcasses; chickens, rabbits, ducks, turkeys, geese and pigs, all hanging from hooks in the open air. Three pigs' heads and two geese were placed above the butcher's block, as if staring at the man's work on the carcasses of their relatives.

The geese always reminded Dickens of Christmas. There was nothing better than a roasted bird dripping with fat on a dining table.

The butcher, blood spattered on his once-clean white apron, was sharpening his knives on a wet stone, the rasping sound like the rattle of ghostly chains.

They turned the corner into Campfield and were at once confronted by the elegant columns of a splendid building. 'The Hall of Science, Mr Dickens, founded on the principles of Robert Owen.'

Dickens glanced across at Lizzie Burns. 'Wasn't he a mill owner?'

She blushed.

'He was, Mr Dickens, a most enlightened one. He believed the education, health and wellbeing of the working man was as important as the goods they created,' answered Robert.

They ran up the stairs. They were immediately greeted by a factotum and welcomed generously to the Hall of Science. Inside was a large concert hall and numerous reading and lecture rooms. Dickens noticed a poster for a mesmerist, Spencer Hall, who was to give an exhibition of his art on Saturday.

'I've seen three thousand people here on a Sunday night for a popular speaker like Mr Watt,' said Robert proudly.

'And the fairer sex is allowed to enter?' asked Dickens, looking across at two women engaged in conversation.

'The fairer sex, as you put it, is *encouraged* to enter,' pronounced Lizzie firmly.

They walked on past another group of people, listening to a speaker talking about the poetry of Byron and Shelley. 'Most of these people are working, are they not?'

'Most work in the mills or warehouses hereabouts.'

'If they are working long hours, how do they find the time to come here?'

'How can they not find the time, Mr Dickens? Men—'

'And women,' interrupted Lizzie.

'—are not succoured by food and drink alone. If the working man is to achieve the aims of the Charter…'

'Universal suffrage?'

'That is the main demand, yes, but there are others. If they are to achieve it, only education can help. Only education can set mankind free. And not just the study of books, Mr Dickens, but of who and what he is.'

They walked past one room. Dickens could hear the sound of raised voices. Robert pushed open the door and the sound of a Christmas carol filled the air around them.

The choir was arrayed on a balcony overlooking a meeting room that looked more like a small chapel than anything else.

A conductor in the well of the room maintained the tempo with a firm stroke of his baton.

*HARK! the Herald Angels sing
Glory to the new-born King!
Peace on Earth, and Mercy mild,
God and Sinners reconcil'd.*

*Joyful all ye Nations rise,
Join the Triumphs of the Skies;
Nature rise and worship him,
Who is born at Bethlehem.*

'Isn't it a little early to sing carols?'

'Not if they want to be ready for Christmas,' answered Robert.

Dickens thought of his own preparations; his magic tricks, the trips to the toy shop hunting for presents for the children, the laborious preparation of Christmas pies and cakes and sweetmeats. He loved it all. A time when families came together to celebrate, when want and greed and money were forgotten.

He stood there and listened to the voices offering up praise for the joy of Christmas. Had people forgotten this simple joy? Had people become so obsessed with utility and efficiency that they no longer celebrated Christmas?

*Hail the Heav'n-born Prince of Peace
Hail the Son of Righteousness!
Light and Life around he brings,*

Ris'n with Healing in his Wings.

Mild he lays his Glory by,
Born that Men no more may die;
Born to raise the sons of Earth,
Born to give them second Birth.

Dickens loved the idea of being given a 'second birth'. To rise again from some earth-bound hell and rediscover what it was to be a man.

The voices rose and the music soared to a dramatic end. The carol finished, and the conductor at the front tapped his music stand with a baton. 'A competent rendition, but where is the joy, ladies and gentlemen, where is the joy?'

It was a question Dickens was asking himself.

CHAPTER TWENTY-EIGHT

Wednesday, December 18, 2019
Central Library, Manchester

Jayne strode up to the librarian's desk. 'I wonder if you could help us?'

The woman looked up and smiled.

'We're looking for the links between Charles Dickens and Manchester, particularly his visit here in 1843?'

The woman's smile broadened. 'Dickens? Funny you should ask, I did my dissertation on him at uni. My studies were on *Bleak House*, though.'

'Great, so you can help us?'

She stood up. 'We've got rather a lot of stuff on him. All the books, obviously, plus he's mentioned in quite a few of the Manchester biographies of the time – Edward Watkin, Elizabeth Gaskell, James Crossley, Richard Cobden. His sister lived in Manchester during the 1840s. You could all check all the articles on JSTOR?'

'What's JSTOR?' asked Ronald.

'A depository of academic dissertations, articles and theses. There's lots on Dickens there, you may find what you're looking for.'

'Sounds great.'

'Give me a moment and I'll get all the books for you. You can log on to JSTOR on the computer over there.'

Jayne and Ronald sat down beside the computer as the librarian searched for the correct books. They logged on to the website and in the search area typed in 'Charles Dickens' and 'Manchester'.

There were 743 results.

'That's too many. Let's try searching for "*A Christmas Carol*" and "Manchester",' said Jayne.

Now 121 results.

'Better. Let's start here and then we can expand later if we have to.'

They began reading the first few articles. Most seemed to be general academic studies of Dickens that mentioned *A Christmas Carol*. After they had read eleven articles and found nothing of interest, the librarian returned carrying a pile of books.

'These are what we have on hand. They are mainly biographies and memoirs of the leading citizens of Manchester during the period. Plus a few biographies of Dickens we have, including the first one written by his friend, John Forster, in the year after he died.'

Jayne stared at the mountain of books. 'Ronald, do you feel comfortable checking out the articles while I go through the books?'

Ronald nodded, still staring at the screen.

Jayne found space on the table and began going through the old books one by one, checking in the index for references to 'Duckworth' ,'1843', or 'Charles Dickens'.

After ten books, she had merely confirmed what she already knew. Dickens was in Manchester in October 1843, and he had made a speech at the Athenaeum but there was no mention of a Robert Duckworth.

She picked up the eleventh book, *Dickens: Interviews and Recollections,* published in 1981. It was a book of contemporary accounts of Dickens' life and work. She flicked through it and finally found gold. An account of the meeting at the Athenaeum by Sir Edward Watkin MP, who was a Director of the Institution. She read it through quickly looking for the name of Robert Duckworth.

Nothing.

She read it again more slowly. Dickens shared the stage that evening with Watkin, Benjamin Disraeli – who later became Prime Minister but was then just another journalist – Richard Cobden, the radical politician, and a man called James Crossley.

Where had she heard that name before?

Hadn't Ronald said he found Crossley's colophon in the back of the first edition?

She whispered to him, 'Come and look at this.'

He left the computer and read the passage. 'That's the man whose mark I found.'

The librarian joined them. 'You're interested in James Crossley?'

'It looks like he could be a link to our Robert Duckworth.'

'Crossley was an avid book collector in Manchester in the 1840s. He founded the Chetham Society in 1843—'

'The same year as Dickens came here,' said Jayne, raising her voice. 'Would Dickens have visited Chetham's Library?'

'Probably, if he knew Crossley. Chetham's and the Portico were the main research and lending libraries at the time. The John Rylands Library didn't open until 1900, and we weren't even on the drawing board.'

'Would they have a visitors book or something like that?' asked Ronald.

'Perhaps. I can ring and ask if you want? They close at four thirty, though.'

Jayne checked the time. It was 3.55 p.m. 'It's okay, we'll go there – it's only ten minutes' walk from here. And if there is a visitors book and if Dickens signed it, perhaps Robert Duckworth will be there too.'

'That's an awful lot of "ifs" and "perhaps", Mrs Sinclair.'

'We've found out as much as we ever will here, Ronald. You need the information by tomorrow evening. We'd better check it out now.'

He stood up. 'What are we waiting for?'

Jayne thanked the librarian and ran out of the library with Ronald trailing in her wake.

Would they get there in time?

CHAPTER TWENTY-NINE

October 5, 1843
Manchester

Dickens checked his watch once more. 4.30 p.m. He should really go back and change before his speech. He did, after all, have a reputation to maintain as a well-dressed man.

'I should return to my hotel. Thank you for your tour of Manchester. It was most... enlightening.'

'We'll walk back with you,' said Robert.

'That will not be necessary, I'm sure I can find my own way back.'

'The streets would not be safe,' said Lizzie, 'and we know the back ways and back alleys. It'll be quicker.'

They left the Hall of Science and marched back up Deansgate, turning right along Peter Street.

They passed an eating house, the windows filled with a feast of savoury pies, huge legs of pork with sage and onion stuffing, long lengths of sausage, most of which seemed to be the colour of the deepest night. Everywhere the air was filled with the aroma of cooked meat, so strong as to form the first course of any meal.

Dickens felt the pangs of hunger. Luckily, the Athenaeum was providing a meal before his speech.

Robert Duckworth had been quiet for a while, with Lizzie acting as the guide. 'On the right is St Peter's Field, the site of the charge of the militia in 1819. Sixty thousand men, women and children gathered on the field that day to listen to Henry Hunt. Nineteen never left it.'

As if finally reaching a decision, Robert spoke. 'It would do me an honour, Mr Dickens, if you would visit my humble home. My wife and children would be most interested in meeting the celebrated author.'

He waited for Dickens to answer, his right hand trembling slightly. Dickens thought of the time. Would he be able to go back and change and still get to the Athenaeum?

He saw the look on the young man's face. 'I would be delighted, Mr Duckworth, but first I think we need to do something.'

Robert's shoulders fell.

'I think we need to take some food back with us. I'm sure your family would really appreciate a bite to eat at a time like this, and after our long walk, I'm more than a little peckish myself.'

Dickens retraced his steps to the eating house, buying from the owner two cheese and onion pies, one steak and kidney pudding, three sweet pies and a leg of roast pork.

'It's too much, Mr Dickens, we'll never eat all of that,' pleaded Robert.

'Well, save some for tomorrow.'

The owner packed the pies in a large hamper and gave it to Robert to carry. They walked back to St Peter's Field, turning into a courtyard on Newberry Street. Robert Duckworth's home was on the ground floor in the middle of a row of terraced houses.

The rooms were small and sparsely furnished. A bed pushed to one corner, a coarse wooden table, three chairs and a fire burning in a large hearth.

Robert's wife, Mary, was surprised to see her husband and even more surprised to see he was accompanied by Charles Dickens.

'You should have told me you were bringing Mr Dickens, Robert,' she said, adjusting her cotton cap.

Dickens noticed a child sitting in the corner, unmoving. Next to him a young girl was helping him build a tower of wooden letters

'Our son, Tom. He's not strong. The doctors can do nothing for him. And our daughter, Charlotte.' The boy merely nodded his head, while the young girl stood up and made a pretty curtsey.

Dickens sat on the floor next to them both. 'What are you playing with?'

'My toys,' answered the young boy.

A set of bricks with letters were piled up in front of him, forming a triangle of words. Dickens could see what the lad had built: 'God Bless us, every one.'

'Good words and an even better sentiment. Now, we have brought some pies to eat. Would you like one?'

The boy and his sister both nodded eagerly. Robert came round and hoisted the young boy on to his shoulders.

For the next hour, they talked and laughed and ate and played, Dickens once again performing his magic tricks to the amazement of all.

It was Robert who finally reminded him of the time. 'It's been like Christmas for us, Mr Dickens, but it's time you returned to your hotel.'

Dickens checked his watch. 'Damn it, I'm late. Time to be going. Thank you, Mary, for a wonderful time. And thank you, Charlotte and Tiny Tom, for being very able magical assistants. You have fine careers ahead of you.

There is no need to see me back to the hotel. I will find a cab.'

'Not around here you won't,' snorted Lizzie. 'I'll walk you back.'

'Tom is coming too,' said Robert, hoisting him on his shoulder. 'He likes to go out of an evening.'

After saying his thanks and his goodbyes once more, Dickens followed Lizzie and Robert and the boy through the dark streets of Manchester, being jostled by the crowds of men, women and children having just left their shifts at the factories.

It was late when Dickens reached the Adelphi. The carriage was already waiting to take him to the Athenaeum.

On the steps of the hotel, Dickens shook Robert's hand warmly. 'Thank you for showing me Manchester.'

'It was my pleasure. There's a lot wrong with it, but it's still my home, Mr Dickens.'

'I hope you find a position soon.'

'I'm sure I will, Mr Dickens. Mrs Gaskell has promised to help me.'

'Goodbye, Tiny Tom, I hope you get better.'

'God bless you, sir,' whispered the boy.

'And thank you too, Lizzie.'

The woman simply grunted a reply.

Dickens turned and vanished inside the hotel. Time to get changed quickly.

But what of the speech. Did he also have time to change it?

CHAPTER THIRTY

Wednesday, December 18, 2019
Manchester

Jayne Sinclair ran to the gatehouse at the entrance to the Chetham's campus. On the left was the world-famous college and music school, and across the car park, the library itself.

The guard checked their ID and reminded them the library would be closing in twenty minutes. Two pupils edged past them carrying large music cases.

'Is the archivist in today?' asked Jayne, crossing her fingers. Ronald was breathing heavily beside her, he really was out of breath after only a short run down Cross Street, past Exchange Square and the National Football Museum.

'He's still here, I think. Do you want me to ring him?'

'If you could, we'd love to see him very quickly.'

The guard rang through. 'He'll see you in the reading room, but he only has ten minutes as they have to clear everyone before they can close.'

'No worries, we'll be done by then.'

Jayne and Ronald walked past the barrier and through the narrow entrance to the open courtyard.

Immediately they were transported to another world. Double-storeyed medieval buildings with mullioned windows, all constructed from a warm sandstone.

In front, a careful manicured lawn led to a small arched door.

Jayne felt like she had just stepped back in time. The contrast between the modern concrete and plate glass of the giant buildings behind them in the city and the elegant proportions of Chetham's couldn't have been more stark.

For a second, she found herself back in the past; scholars striding across the courtyard, struggling against the winds coming off the river, their gowns floating like bats' wings. Young boys in high, ruffled collars, baggy pantaloons and top hats running as they were late for class. And Dickens himself, dandy that he was, vanishing through the low door into the library, accompanied by friends, a woman waiting outside.

Just as suddenly, the image faded and Jayne was back in the present.

'What's up? We need to be quick to meet the archivist,' said Ronald, hurrying into the library.

Jayne shook her head to clear it. These visions were fewer and fewer these days, but it always felt as if the past were reaching out to talk to her when it happened.

She ran after Ronald and bumped into him as he stopped in the doorway, staring up at the books in their locked and barred bookcases.

'Heaven,' he whispered. 'I could lose myself in here for years.'

'You can, but perhaps another time.' Jayne ushered him up the stairs. At the top, they were greeted by rows of dark, almost blackened, wooden bookcases stretching the length of the room. Above each bookcase, the subject matter contained beneath was written in gold paint.

'Mrs Sinclair, I presume.'

A tall, elegant man stood at the entrance to the reading room on the right.

'That's right. You must be the archivist?'

'My name is Randall. How can I help you today?'

'Myself and Ronald Welsh,' she looked behind her, but Ronald was just staring at the books, his mouth wide open, 'were wondering if we could ask you a few questions. We are researching Charles Dickens and his visits to Manchester, particularly in 1843.'

'And you were wondering if we had a visitors' book which he signed?'

Jayne smiled. 'Right first time, how did you know?'

'It's a common question. I'm afraid we did have a visitors' book and Charles Dickens probably did visit Chetham's...' The man paused.

'There sounds like a big "but" coming now.'

'You are correct. The visitors' books have been lost somewhere, so we have no records. Sorry to disappoint you.'

Jayne felt the air leave her lungs and her shoulders sagged. Her hopes had been built up but now they had been so easily dashed.

'From diaries and other sources, we can confirm that Benjamin Franklin and Karl Marx spent some time here, if that's any help. We also know Dickens was acquainted with James Crossley and the librarian at the time, Mr Jones, but I'm afraid there is no documentary proof of him visiting Chetham's.'

'What about a man called Robert Duckworth? He was living in Manchester in 1843 too.'

Mr Randall cocked his head. 'Duckworth? The name doesn't ring a bell. Was he a member of the Chetham's Society?'

'We don't know. We just know he was linked to Dickens in 1843.'

'I'm sorry, I can't help you. I'll check in the minutes of the society to see if there is any mention of a Mr Duckworth if you want.'

'Thank you, that would be useful.'

'We do have the catalogue for the Crossley sale though.'

Jayne frowned. 'Catalogue? Sale?'

'After James Crossley died his complete library was put up for auction. Many individuals and other libraries bought his rare collection of books. I can check it now if you want?'

'That would be great.'

He walked into the main body of the library, returning a minute later.

'That was quick,' said Jayne.

'I knew where it was located.'

'Do you know exactly where all the books are?' asked Ronald.

'Most of them.'

'Cool,' whispered Ronald.

He went into the reading room and placed the book on a wooden lectern standing on the large round table in the centre. 'The books are in listed in alphabetical order by author. A clumsy way of cataloguing but common at that time.'

As he turned the page, his fingers traced the names written in the column on the left. He reached the 'Ds' and slowed down, checking more carefully.

'I'm sorry, there don't seem to be any Dickens books in the catalogue of sale.'

'Isn't that strange?' asked Jayne, 'I thought Dickens was one of the most popular authors at that time.'

'Possibly. But James Crossley could have sold or given away the Dickens books before his death. Or he may have simply not wanted to have such a popular writer in his collection. I suppose we'll never know.'

He checked his watch. 'If there is nothing else, I'm afraid we need to close the library now.'

Jayne sighed. 'Thank you for your time, Mr Randall,' she said, and turned to go, putting her arm over Ronald's shoulder.

They walked towards the stairs, but then Ronald turned back. 'Can I come here again and look at the books?'

'Of course, Mr Welsh. Just call me to make an appointment. Which books would you like to see?'

Ronald thought for a moment. 'All of them.'

CHAPTER THIRTY-ONE

Wednesday, December 18, 2019
Manchester

After leaving Chetham's, they both stood outside for a while, the rush-hour traffic starting to build up on the road beside them.

'I was sure we'd find the link here,' said Jayne.

'It's just past four thirty. What do we now, Mrs Sinclair? The auction is tomorrow.'

For once in her life, Jayne was stumped. 'We've seen all of the documentary evidence at Central Library. There are still the parish registers, but they won't show us a link to Charles Dickens. Chetham's has nothing and the Lancashire and Cheshire archives won't have anything either.

I'll check them once more online when I go home, but I doubt if anything to help us exists.'

'So where do we go next?'

'I don't think there is anywhere else to go, Ronald. All the archives will be closing around now.'

'So that's it, we're just going to give up?'

Jayne Sinclair gritted her teeth. 'Listen, Ronald, if there was anywhere else to go, anything else to search, I would do it. Give me more time and we can probably find him, but—'

'We don't have more time, Mrs Sinclair, the auction is tomorrow.'

'Don't you think I already know? What do you suggest we do?'

Ronald looked down at his feet, shuffling from side to side, playing with a small stone he had found on the pavement. 'I don't know,' he finally said quietly.

'Look, I'll have a think if there is anything else once I get home. There is still tomorrow morning. The auction isn't until the evening, isn't that right?'

'Yeah, 6.30 pm because of the time difference with America.'

'So we have till tomorrow. I'll see what I can dig up tonight.'

'Okay,' he said softly.

Jayne pointed back over her shoulder. 'Can I give you a lift home? I'm afraid the car is parked near Oxford Road.'

'No. I think I'll go back to Central Library. Perhaps the JSTOR articles will have something.'

'But you've read over a hundred of them.'

'There were 751 articles in our first search, I still haven't checked them all out.'

'It's a waste of time, Ronald.'

'It's my time to waste, Mrs Sinclair.'

Jayne shrugged her shoulders. For a second she was tempted to go back with him, but he wouldn't discover anything. Search engines were so efficient these days, a result would have come up already. 'You might want to come at it from a different angle.'

'What's that?'

'Just search for "Robert Duckworth" and see what comes up. I googled the name before and there was nothing relevant. JSTOR may find something, though.'

'Okay, I'll give it a go. Call me later.'

She nodded and he walked off, before stopping for a second and then turning back. 'I thought about what you said when we first met. I've decided to give my half share of the proceeds from the auction to the homeless charity where I bought the book.'

Jayne was surprised. 'Fifteen thousand pounds is a lot of money, Ronald.'

He held out his arms. 'What's money to me, Mrs Sinclair?'

'It's a lot of tomato soup.'

'I have enough. I always have enough. But if we could find out who Robert Duckworth was, then I would be able to give forty-five thousand pounds. That would be much better, wouldn't it?'

'It would, Ronald. Thirty thousand pounds better.'

CHAPTER THIRTY-TWO

October 5, 1843
The Adelphi Hotel, Manchester

Back in his room, Dickens removed his walking clothes, changed his shirt and selected the bright yellow waistcoat and a matching green baize coat.

'It should set the right tone for my speech,' he said out loud, checking himself in the mirror.

He read through his speech once more.

Dear Friends and Colleagues,

It gives me great pleasure to give a speech at the consecration of this temple to learning; the Athenaeum. Here, it is hoped the residents of Manchester will discover the glories, knowledge, power and beauty of books and reading. They may even discover my own worthless attempts at literature…

His face fell. After everything he had seen, it would not do. How could he let his audience down with such a bland choice of phrase? How could he not let them know what he had seen? How could he not at least acknowledge the divisions he had seen in this new city?

He picked up his pen, selected a sheet of paper from the desk and began writing.

Ladies and gentlemen, I am sure I need scarcely tell you that I am very proud and happy; and that I take it as a great distinction to be asked to come amongst you on an occasion such as this, when, even with the brilliant and beautiful spectacle which I see before me, I can hail it as the most brilliant and beautiful circumstance of all, that we assemble together here, even here, upon neutral ground, where we have no more knowledge of party difficulties, or public animosities between side and side, or between man and man, than if we were a public meeting in the commonwealth of Utopia.

That was a better beginning. At least he now acknowledged the difficulties Manchester had suffered over the last couple of years. The rest of his speech might not be what his audience wanted to hear, but it's what they should hear.

And if he didn't say it, who would?

CHAPTER THIRTY-THREE

October 5, 1843
The Athenaeum, Manchester

'Where have you been, Charles? We've all been waiting and you've missed dinner. Disraeli has nearly finished his speech and you are on next.'

'I had to re-draft the speech at the hotel, Harrison. I'm sorry but I am here now.'

His friend pushed him on to the stage, towards an empty chair. As he walked across the candlelit auditorium, a whisper ran through the audience followed by sustained applause.

Disraeli paused for a moment, smiled and then carried on as if nothing had happened. Dickens sat down next to the Chairman, Edward Watkin.

The man, who smelt strongly of tobacco, leant across and whispered, 'You're the next speaker, Mr Dickens. I'll introduce you and then you begin.'

Dickens nodded.

Disraeli continued for a few minutes more, before ending on a rousing note and sitting down.

Watkin stood up and began his introduction in a deep voice, with the soft vowels of the Shropshire countryside buried deep within it.

Dickens listened to the applause, gazing out at the audience. It was an interesting mix of people. At the front sat the great and good of Manchester; the prosperous businessmen and their even more prosperous-looking wives.

To the right was seated Mrs Gaskell and her husband, accompanied by other stiff and stern men dressed in black clerical garb. The local congregation of the Unitarians, no doubt.

Behind them was the main body of the audience; clerks and working men, engineers and seamstresses, shop workers and trade representatives. The very people for whom the Athenaeum had been created, here to hear him.

This was the largest audience he had spoken to so far, but instead of being nervous, he felt exhilarated. As if this stage was the place he was always meant to be.

Mr Watkin finished his introduction and there was a thunderous round of applause that continued for more than a minute. Dickens stood up and took a small bow, advancing to the front of the stage so that all may see him.

Standing there, all eyes upon him, he decided to speak from the heart. To tell these people what he really believed, and what, after his guided tour of the city, he felt was important.

After reading from his notes at the beginning, he discarded them, placing them ostentatiously inside his pocket.

Perhaps a little flattery would soften the message. He grasped his lapel and began speaking.

'It well becomes, particularly well becomes, this enterprising town, this little world of labour, that she should stand out foremost in the foremost rank in such a cause. It well becomes her that, among her numerous and noble public institutions, she should have a splendid temple sacred to the education and improvement of a large class of those who, in their various useful stations, assist in the production of our wealth, and in rendering her name famous through the world.'

There was a smattering of applause at the compliment. He stopped allowing the clapping to die down, enjoying the moment. 'I think it is grand to know that, while her factories re-echo with the clanking of stupendous engines, and the whirl and rattle of machinery, the immortal mechanism of God's own hand, the mind, is not forgotten in the din and uproar, but is lodged and tended in a palace of its own.'

He waved to indicate the building around them and was rewarded with another round of applause. After detailing the financial straits the Athenaeum had suffered over the last few years, he decided to plunge into the meat of his argument.

'How often have we heard from a large class of men, wise in their generation, who would really seem to be born and bred for no other purpose than to pass into currency counterfeit and mischievous scraps of wisdom, as it is the sole pursuit of some other criminals to utter base coin – how often have we heard from them, as an all-convincing argument, that "a little learning is a dangerous thing"?'

He glanced across at Silas Grindley, who was sitting in the front row. The man scowled. Dickens carried on, his voice dripping with sarcasm.

'Why, a little hanging was considered a very dangerous thing, according to the same authorities, with this difference that, because a little hanging was dangerous, we had a great deal of it; and because a little learning was dangerous, we were to have none at all.'

The audience laughed dutifully. Behind him, he heard Mr Watkin shift uncomfortably in his seat. Silas Grindley continued to scowl.

'Why, when I hear such cruel absurdities gravely reiterated, I do sometimes begin to doubt whether the parrots of society are not more pernicious to its interests than its birds of prey. I should be glad to hear such people's estimate of the comparative danger of "a little learning" and a vast amount of ignorance; I should be glad to know which they consider the most prolific parent of misery and crime. Descending a little lower in the social scale, I should be glad to assist them in their calculations, by carrying them into certain gaols and nightly refuges I know of, where my own heart dies within me, when I see thousands of immortal creatures condemned, without alternative or choice, to tread not what our great poet calls the "primrose path" to the everlasting bonfire, but one of jaded flints and stones, laid down by brutal ignorance, and held together, like the solid rocks, by years of this most wicked axiom.'

He was quite pleased with this little metaphor. He could see the workmen and shopkeepers leaning forward to listen more intently. The mill owners, bankers and rentiers were glancing across at each other suspiciously. Had they invited a viper into their midst?

Probably, but he did not care. He owed it to Robert Duckworth and his family, and even to Lizzie Burns, to plunge on.

'And this I know, that the first unpurchasable blessing earned by every man who makes an effort to improve himself in such a place as the Athenaeum, is self-respect – an inward dignity of character which, once acquired and righteously maintained, nothing – no, not the hardest drudgery, nor the direst poverty – can vanquish. Though he should find it hard for a season even to keep the wolf – hunger – from his door, let him but once have chased the dragon – ignorance – from his hearth, and self-respect and hope are left him. You could no more deprive him of those sustaining qualities by loss or destruction of his worldly goods, than you could by plucking out his eyes, take from him an internal consciousness of the bright glory of the sun.'

The rest of his speech flowed superbly. He felt at one with his audience. They were listening to his every word, hearing in his sentences the truth of what he believed.

Education was the way to set men free.

He paused before delivering the end he had written. Holding the moment in his hands. An actor waiting for the audience to beg him to continue.

'But it is upon a much better and wider scale, let me say it once again – it is in the effect of such institutions upon the great social system, and the peace and happiness of mankind, that I delight to contemplate them; and, in my heart, I am quite certain that long after your institution, and others of the same nature, have crumbled into dust, the noble harvest of the seed sown in them will shine out brightly in the wisdom, the mercy, and the forbearance of another race.'

As man and woman, the audience rose to applaud him. Even the merchants and their wives at the front rose and clapped the sentiments, if not the content of his speech.

He stood there, sweat dripping from his brow, even though it was October, drinking in the adulation.

This is what he lived for. This is what he deserved.

CHAPTER THIRTY-FOUR

Wednesday, December 18, 2019
Didsbury, Manchester

Jayne reached home and immediately was greeted by Mr Smith, her anger and disappointment melting as she stroked his fur.

Throughout the drive she had been thinking if there was anything she had missed, anything she had overlooked.

But there was nothing.

In the time allotted, she had done the best she could.

The realisation didn't help, though. She hated failure more than anything else and, in her mind, in this investigation she had failed.

'It's time to feed you.'

The cat meowed his agreement and padded back to the kitchen with his tail held high, just to remind her where his bowl was.

She went to the fridge and brought out one of his favourites, lamb with vegetables in a rich sauce. He definitely ate better than she did.

She filled his bowl, adding some dry food for the crunch of it, before going back to the fridge to pour herself a large, cold glass of New Zealand Sauvignon Blanc.

As the zesty gooseberry flavours of the wine danced on her tongue, she decided there was one more thing she could do.

She could try to come at it from a different angle. Instead of trying to link Robert Duckworth with Charles Dickens in 1843, what happened if she researched the future lives of her five possible suspects?

She brought out the list once more, checking it against her previous work and re-sorting the names into chronological order. To her eye, it always looked neater that way.

Birth	Address	Family	Job	Residence
1806	Rogers Rd	Elizabeth, 4 children	Calico Printer	Angel Meadow

1811	Minehead St	Sarah, 2 children	Cotton Weaver	Ancoats
1816	Ardwick Green	Helen, 5 children	Block Printer	Ardwick
1817	Halson St	Mary, 4 children	Editor	Chorlton-on- M
1819	Newberry St	Mary, 2 children	Clerk	St Annes

She would now go through the 1851, 1861 and 1871 Censuses again, seeing if there were any links to Charles Dickens or his family in Manchester. Dickens had died in 1869, so she felt that she could cut her search off by then.

She knew it was a long shot, and she had criticised Ronald for wasting his own time, but she had to try something. She couldn't just sit there when there was still time to solve the mystery.

She looked at the first two Robert Duckworths. Both were no longer on the 1861 Census. She cross-referenced their names with the list of births, marriages and deaths, discovering that both they and all of their children had died in 1854. Checking with Google, she found that Manchester had suffered a severe outbreak of cholera in that year. Obviously, the disease had taken away whole families in the overcrowded slums.

The next Robert Duckworth, born in 1816, had survived to the ripe old age of 68, dying in 1884. His family and descendants were numerous in both the 1871 and the 1881 Census, so if he was her man, the Lost Cousins website should throw up quite a few present-day descendants.

The editor, the fourth on her list, she couldn't find in Manchester in 1861, but by broadening the search, she found him and his wife living in Bristol, where he had been working as a teacher. She followed him until 1871, but could find no links to Dickens.

The final Robert Duckworth was in the 1861 Census, living with his wife and one child, a Charles Duckworth. What had happened to the other two children they'd had? She went back through her notes and found their names: Thomas and Charlotte.

There were also two lodgers living with them in 1861. The enumerator had marked a large 'UK' in the space where their names should have been. Unknown. He obviously didn't go back to interview them.

By 1871, they were still living in the same place and the man's profession was still a clerk. Their son, Charles, was now fourteen years old and still a scholar.

By the 1881 Census they had both vanished. In their place a family of six, the Hewitts, occupied the same address. A quick check with Births, Marriages and Deaths showed they had died in 1873 and 1874 respectively.

That was it, then.

It had always been a long shot, researching the Census, but she had hoped something would come up. Now she felt oddly deflated, as if the last semblance of hope had left her body, leaving nothing but emptiness in its place.

It was time to make the call to Michael Underwood.

She dialled his number and he answered in two rings. 'What do you have for me, Jayne?'

'Not a lot, I'm afraid.' She detailed her research over the last few days. 'So we have five possibilities, but I don't know which one it is.'

'That is disappointing. I had high hopes for you, Jayne, and so did Ronald. Anyway, thank you for your work. I'll send you the cheque after I have sold the book.'

He ended the call and Jayne was left holding the phone to her ear.

The cat stretched his front and back legs and strolled over to the patio doors. It was time to let him out for his visit to number nine.

She got up slowly and opened the door.

He shot straight out with a meow for goodbye.

Standing in the doorway, she inhaled the cold night air.

It was exactly a week until Christmas. She had bought no presents, nor had she arranged to do anything. Robert and Vera were going away, so she would be spending Christmas Day on her own.

The realisation worried her. Christmas wasn't a time to be alone, it was a time for fun and joy and happiness.

But not for her, not this year.

She sighed. She couldn't even solve this case. Tomorrow, the auction would take place with nobody being any the wiser who Robert Duckworth was.

He had vanished in the fog of time, like so many people before him.

Would the same happen to her?

The thought made Jayne feel even sadder than before.

CHAPTER THIRTY-FIVE

October 5, 1843
The Adelphi Hotel, Manchester

Dickens finally nestled beneath the covers of his bed, pulling the blanket around him. He was slightly drunk, but the exhilaration he felt after the speech was not just a consequence of the alcohol.

Even Silas Grindley had come up to congratulate him. 'I might not agree with the details, but I can wholeheartedly support the sentiments of your address, Mr Dickens,' he had pronounced in his northern accent, 'so I've decided to open up a free school for the children of my workers when they're at the mill. Somewhere where they can learn whilst their parents are working. Now, what do you think of that?'

Dickens shook his hand forcefully. 'I think it is a wonderful idea, Mr Grindley. I would only hope that other mill owners may follow your example.'

'I'll have a chat with 'em, can't say more than that.'

Dickens chuckled to himself. At least the speech had done some good.

Then he thought for a moment.

One speech in Manchester was fine, but could he do more? He had promised to write a pamphlet in support of Mr Southwood Smith, but a pamphlet would just be another piece of paper, forgotten five minutes after he had written it.

Couldn't he write something more useful? Something that would actually touch people emotionally, as his novels had done?

Something joyful. Something to give people hope.

He remembered the voices from the Hall of Science singing their carols.

Something about Christmas, maybe?

As he drifted off to sleep, the thought stayed with him.

In his dreams he was visited by the ghosts of Christmas past, Christmas present and the Christmases yet to come.

And they spoke to him.

CHAPTER THIRTY-SIX

Thursday, December 19, 2019
Didsbury, Manchester

Jayne sat up straight in bed. The curtains were drawn and the bedroom was dark.

Was that a noise?

She listened intently, straining to pick up the soft steps of a burglar.

Nothing. Just the creaking of the house as it cooled down.

She switched on the light, blinking against its brightness.

What had she been dreaming about?

She struggled to remember. It was hazy, yet at the time it had seemed so vivid; a man dressed in white. Was it Dave Gilmour? Telling her to keep going, never give up. 'Look at the children,' he had said.

But she didn't have any children. It wasn't anything she felt sad about. Instead, it was a conscious decision on her part. She just never felt settled enough with Paul to bring another human being into the world. And he had made it perfectly clear he didn't want their lives destroyed by the arrival of a small, braying monster.

What had the dream meant? 'Look at the children.'

The clock next to her said 4.35 a.m.

Should she get up? Or just go back to sleep?

After a moment's hesitation, she threw back the covers and grabbing a dressing gown to protect her from the cold. Padding downstairs, she switched on the central heating in the hall, hearing the water boiler whirr into action. At least the house would be warm.

Mr Smith was waiting for her in the kitchen.

Well, not exactly waiting for her, more aware of her presence. He steadfastly refused to leave his position, close to the radiator.

She walked over and scratched him behind the ears.

'What time did you come back through the cat flap?'

She received a purr of pleasure in answer.

Whilst the house heated up, she switched on the Nespresso machine and soon the aroma of coffee filled the air. There was something terribly visceral about the smell of freshly brewed coffee, as if it touched some deep sense of comfort buried within her body.

She held the warm mug in the palms of her hands, bringing the steaming liquid up to her face. On the opposite wall, the digital clock showed the date: December 19, 2019.

176 years ago to the day, Charles Dickens had published *A Christmas Carol* for five shillings a copy. Today, one of those first editions would be sold at auction for nearly 30,000 pounds.

That was inflation for you. The price would be even higher if she could find Robert Duckworth. Up to three times more, according to Ronald.

But there was nothing left to research. Sometimes the documentation just didn't exist any more. In this case, even DNA couldn't help find a way of breaking this particular brick wall.

DNA. The link from one generation to the next, passed down from parents to their children. A living link with the past in every person.

Is that what her dream meant? 'Look at the children.' Was her subconscious telling her to check out the children of each of the Robert Duckworths?

She checked the clock again: 4.45 a.m.

Outside, Manchester was still dark. It was nearly the winter equinox, the shortest day in the calendar where the sun barely kisses the sky before it sinks once more below the horizon.

What did she have to lose?

She had heard nothing from Ronald last night. He would have called if he had found anything. It was probably a wild-goose chase, but the nagging doubt still remained in her mind. If she didn't check it out, the suspicion would still remain she hadn't done everything possible.

She switched on her computer and, while it booted up, made herself another coffee and fed the cat. He, of course, managed to leave the comfort of a warm radiator for a bowl of lamb's liver and gravy. He could never resist food.

She sat down and began researching the children of the Robert Duckworths, starting from the top.

Five hours and four more cups of coffee later, she struck gold.

In the 1861 Census, she discovered that Charlotte Duckworth, the daughter of the fifth Robert Duckworth, was at one time working as a servant to Elizabeth Gaskell, the writer, and her husband, William, in their house in Plymouth Grove, just off Oxford Road.

Was that the link?

She vaguely remembered studying Mrs Gaskell in school. Didn't she write the book on which that wonderful TV series was based – *Cranford*?

According to Wikipedia, Elizabeth Gaskell was a celebrated writer by 1861, having published *Mary Barton*, *North and South*, *Cranford* and a biography of Charlotte Brontë. She even wrote short stories about Christmas for *Household Words*, the magazine edited by Charles Dickens.

There it was.

There was the link, she knew it in her bones.

'Calm down, Jayne, don't rush it, do the work. What about the other children?'

She went back to the list she had created for this Robert Duckworth's children.

Robert Duckworth	**1819**
Mary Duckworth	**1815**
Thomas Duckworth	**1837**
Charlotte Duckworth	**1840**
Charles Duckworth	**1854**

'It looks like they started a family and then stopped, having another child thirteen years later and calling him Charles.'

The cat stared at her as she spoke out loud.

She searched the 1861 Census but could find no reference for a Thomas Duckworth in Manchester. The BMD index did show a death in 1854, but unless she obtained the certificate, she wouldn't know if this was the same person.

Had he died or just moved somewhere else?

She didn't know now, but she would check it out later.

What about Charles Duckworth? The name rang a bell, didn't it?

Then it hit her.

She thought about Vera's ancestry chart. Didn't she have a relative called Charles Duckworth?

The file was in its usual place, and there it was in the 1901 Census. A Charles Duckworth, living with Vera's great-grandfather. She had even written herself a note to check up on this man.

Thomas Henry Duckworth	1879 -1924
Eliza Duckworth	1874 -1931
Margaret Duckworth	1899 -????
Samuel Duckworth	1901 -????
Francis Duckworth	1903 -1966
Hermione Duckworth	1905 -????
Charles Duckworth	1854 -????

Excited now, she brought up the 1881 Census and typed in 'Charles Duckworth'.

There he was, living in Manchester with his wife Eliza, and just one child: Thomas Henry Duckworth.

Jayne punched the air and shouted, 'Get in.'

Mr Smith stared at her with utter disdain, embarrassed to have such a human as a housemate.

So Vera was related to this man; he was her great-great-grandfather. At least now she could push Vera's family chart back to 1819. With a bit of luck, and a lot of digging in the Manchester parish registers, she should be able to take it back even further.

She laid out all her findings in front of her. Robert Duckworth's daughter, Charlotte, had been employed as a servant in Elizabeth Gaskell's house. Gaskell was closely linked to Charles Dickens, even writing short stories for him in his magazine.

And then the realisation dawned on her.

She still hadn't proved a connection between Charles Dickens and Robert Duckworth. There was a possibility of a link through Elizabeth Gaskell, but that was all.

There was no direct documentary proof. And, without evidence, it was all wishful thinking.

She remembered one of Sergeant McNally's lectures. 'Putting a criminal away is about three things. Evidence. Evidence. Evidence. If you don't find the evidence, the case won't stand up in a court of law.'

The truth was, she had no evidence.

Her shoulders slumped and she leant her head against her desk, feeling the coolness of the Formica against her forehead. All that work for nothing.

Just then, her mobile phone rang.

CHAPTER THIRTY-SEVEN

Thursday, December 19, 2019
Didsbury, Manchester

'Mrs Sinclair?'

It was Ronald, his voice tired as if he hadn't slept last night.

'Good morning, Ronald. I have some good news and some good news.'

'The good news first this time.'

'I think I know which Robert Duckworth received the book...'

'That's great, Mrs Sinclair.' The voice on the other end of the line was suddenly full of energy.

Jayne felt sorry at bringing him back down to earth. ' The bad news is, I just can't prove it.'

She went on to describe her work on the Censuses and the link to Elizabeth Gaskell.

The voice was excited again. 'I read many articles about Dickens and Mrs Gaskell. They had a very close relationship, and he even suggested the title of one of her books, *North and South*.'

'That's great, Ronald, but it still doesn't prove a link between Dickens and Robert Duckworth. We just haven't found any evidence.'

There was silence at the other end of the phone for a long time.

'Ronald?' Jayne enquired.

'I'm thinking, Mrs Sinclair. You know, Mrs Gaskell retained most of her letters. I think the archive is stored at John Rylands Library.'

'Could there be documentation in the archive?'

'It's worth a shot, we have no other ideas, do we? The auction isn't for another nine hours. We still have time to look.'

Why not? Jayne thought. If she didn't check it out, she would spend the rest of her life worrying that she had missed something. 'Let me call the archivist to reserve a place to take a look at the Gaskell letters. Meet me outside the John Rylands Library in Deansgate at…' she checked the clock on the wall, 'eleven o' clock.'

'I'll be there. And Mrs Sinclair? I feel good about this one.'

CHAPTER THIRTY-EIGHT

Thursday, December 19, 2019
John Rylands Library, Manchester

Jayne drove like a bat out of hell to get to Deansgate.

She had been rushing around since she had finished the call with Ronald, calling John Rylands Library immediately After explaining to the archivist about the Dickens first edition, the link to Robert Duckworth, his sister working for Elizabeth Gaskell, and the urgency of the auction, the archivist waived the usual twenty-four hours notice of requests, and reserved a place in the Research Room for them.

Jayne then completed the membership form online, spending another twenty minutes going through the catalogue requesting all items that could have a possible connection to Charles Dickens. There were a lot of documents and letters as Dickens had published articles and stories by Mrs Gaskell in the magazines he edited, and had advised her on the publication of her early novels.

All this had taken time, however. Ronald was already waiting in front of the library as she arrived at fifteen minutes past eleven. 'You're here Mrs Sinclair, I was beginning to get worried for a moment.'

'Traffic was bad and parking was worse. Shall we go in?'

For a moment, she paused and looked up at the imposing Gothic front of the building.

It looked more like a church than a library with dark red sandstone, stained-glass oriel windows, lacy tracery and finely detailed carving. A temple to the religion of learning, she thought.

They hurried round the side to a modern extension and spotted a receptionist behind a desk.

'Where can I find the Research Room?'

'You have reserved a seat?'

'Correct.'

'Go up to Level 4, the lift is over there. Reader Reception'

'Thank you.' They took the lift and found themselves in a modern room with an array of oak desks occupied by researchers.

'I have reserved two chairs.'

The reader receptionist checked his computer. 'Mrs Sinclair?'

'That's right.'

'Do you have photo ID and proof of address?'

Jayne produced her driving licence and an electricity bill.

'Perfect. You have been assigned chairs 12 and 13. The archivist will bring the documents to the Issue Desk, you can pick them up from there. You can deposit your bags and coat in the lockers, they're not allowed in the research room. Plus all notes must be taken in pencil. You can of course use a laptop if you have one.'

'How long will the documents be?'

'About twenty minutes, she's usually very quick.'

'Thank you.'

'They went back to the lockers and Jayne deposited her bag and coat inside. Ronald kept wearing his jacket. She could see he was self-conscious about taking it off.

'Come on, I want to show you something while we wait for the documents.'

They took the lift down but instead of going down to the lobby, they entered the main Reading Room of the Library. Even more than the exterior, the interior of the room resembled a cathedral. The constant noise of Manchester had vanished, replaced by the quiet of a cloister. High stained glass windows gave a clear, clerical light while statues of academic luminaries were the saints of learning. A red carpeted aisle down the centre was dominated by an arched tracery roof soaring thirty feet above their heads.

And of course, there were books, thousands of them, arrayed in solid oak bookshelves on either side of the central aisle and on a mezzanine floor above.

'It's beautiful,' said Ronald, his mouth open staring at the books and the ceiling.

'I thought you'd like it. Ages since I've been here, I often think of it as one of the hidden gems of Manchester.'

'Who created it?'

'A woman, Enriqueta Rylands, the widow of a wealthy mill owner and merchant, John Rylands. It was opened in 1900 as a temple to learning.'

On either side, in small alcoves, people were sitting and studying, taking notes in pencil.

Ronald was now circling around slowly, giving himself a 360 degree view of the library. 'I could spend my life here,' he whispered.

'Not possible, I'm afraid. I wouldn't mind either though.' She touched him on the shoulder. 'Let's go back upstairs. With a bit of luck, the letters and documents will be ready for us.'

They returned to Research Room and, as Jayne had predicted, the archivist was waiting for them at the Issue Desk.

'Here are the boxes you requested. Please keep them in order and return them to the issue desk when you are finished. If you need anything, please don't hesitate to ask.' She smiled checking that they had understood.

'You'll also need these.' She held up two pairs of nitrile gloves. 'Please put them on before touching the letters. There's a book rest for reading the documents in the table. I hope you find what you're looking for. A link between *A Christmas Carol,* Manchester and Mrs Gaskell would be lovely.'

Jayne had told her the reason for the urgency. It was the only reason they had managed to get in so quickly. 'I hope so too.'

Jayne and Ronald carried everything to their desk. 'Time to cross our fingers,' Jayne said putting on the gloves, 'the evidence is in these letters or else we have nothing left. Shall we read them together?'

'Go ahead,' nodded Ronald leaning forward as Jayne opened the first box, removing the letter on top.

The paper was thick and the ink, in Dickens' flowing, exuberant hand, with a strong slant to the left, had already turned to a dark brown, earth colour.

They both read the first line of the letter, Ronald's lips moving as he did.

My dear Mrs Gaskell…

CHAPTER THIRTY-NINE

October 6, 1843
On the train to Birmingham.

Dickens pulled out a notebook and requested a pen and ink from the steward. It wasn't going to be easy writing on the moving train as it rocked from side to side, but he feared if he didn't do it now, the ideas he had dreamt last night would vanish like the morning mist in a woodland dell.

He had woken late, rushed his breakfast and picked up the bag the valet had packed. Just as he was about to leave, Fanny had arrived with the children and their maids to see him off

'We'll ride together. Harry and Charles so want to see the trains.' She leant in closer. 'Between you and me, I think the wits will be scared out of them by the engines, but they still want to go to the station.'

Dickens tousled Harry's hair. 'Brave boy.'

The climbed into the cab called by the hotel and, all six jammed together, rattled off to the station.

Dickens stared out of the window for a moment before looking back at his sister. 'Are you happy here, Fanny?'

She made a little moue with her mouth. It was one of the most endearing things about his sister, he thought, the way she had of pursing her lips when asked a question. How he would miss her.

'I think I am, Charles. I miss the family, of course, and mother, but Henry is a good man and the children love it here.'

'Do you miss your singing? You wanted to sing opera…'

'That,' she smiled, 'it was just a young girl's dream.'

'Sometimes, we should hang onto our dreams even when we're grown up. What's your dream, Harry?'

The boy thought for a moment. 'I'd like walk to school, on my own.'

Dickens looked at his sister. She shook her head.

'I'm sure the doctors will be able to help you achieve your dream. When I go back to London, I will look for a special doctor to see if he can cure you. You must come to our house for Christmas and meet him. Would you like that?'

The boy nodded his head vigorously.

He turned back to speak directly to his sister. 'I mean it, I would love you and the family to spend Christmas with us.'

Before she could answer, the cabbie shouted. 'We is here.'

Now he was attempting to write on the moving train. His normal strong handwriting, cramped and shaky.

Harry must be in the Christmas book, and Robert Duckworth's son. Too many children suffered in this world while their pain was ignored.

Grindley needed to be in there too, or at least his ideas, the man himself was too much of this world. Perhaps, make him older, more alone and more misanthropic, with a partner who had died years ago called Marley.

The ghosts should make an appearance, shadowing the main character, and showing him the errors of his ways. What should he call the misanthropic man? He vaguely remembered a name on a tombstone in Edinburgh when he had visited that city. Scrooge wasn't it? A perfect name for a miser.

Of course, Robert had to be in there. A clerk for the miser. A good man with a young family one of whom was severely ill.

There was something here, something he could work with.

He stared out of the train at the countryside of England as it raced past his window.

A book to remind people of the wonder of Christmas and offer them hope for a better future. a chance for rebirth and redemption whatever they had done in the past or the present.

That was it. A book to offer hope.

But what was he going to call it?

The memory of the smiling faces of his sister's family and of the people in the Hall of Science as they sang, swam into his mind.

A Christmas Carol.

That's not a bad title. With the chapters divided into staves like a hymn.

He sat back and planned the opening sentence in his mind. Something to confuse and astound, to introduce the ghosts and the idea of redemption.

He scribbled the words quickly in his notebook.

Marley was dead, to begin with. There is no doubt whatever about that. The register of his burial was signed by the clergyman, the clerk, the undertaker, and the chief mourner.

It wasn't bad, a start anyway.

The beginning of a story was always the most difficult. Often, a writer didn't know where the beginning was until he had written the whole story. At other times, the beginnings came quickly as a half-formed image, almost dream-like.

This one felt correct.

A good beginning.

CHAPTER FORTY

Thursday, December 19, 2019
John Rylands Library, Manchester

After three hours they had read all the letters without finding a single reference to Robert Duckworth.

They both slumped back in their chairs in the Research Room whispering to each other, reluctant to disturb the church-like atmosphere.

'What do we do now?' asked Ronald.

Jayne shook her head. 'I don't know. But I need something to eat and a coffee to give a jolt to my brain. We'll return the box to the archivist and go to the cafe downstairs.'

'Do we have to? Can't we stay here?' He glanced around the room. 'It's peaceful here.'

'We need to talk, Ronald, we can't spend our lives whispering and I need food for my stomach as well as my soul.'

Reluctantly, Ronald followed her to the cafe after they had returned the documents to the issue desk.

'Did you find your Robert Duckworth?' asked the archivist.

Jayne shook her head. 'He seems to have vanished off the face of the earth, there's not even a reference to his daughter.'

'It's not surprising, domestic servants did not have a prominent place in literary affairs in that era. There are other boxes in the Gaskell collection you could look at.'

'Thank you, but we need a break to re-group and re-think, and to grab some food.'

'When you're ready, let me know how I can help you later.'

Downstairs, in the cafe, Jayne ordered a salmon quiche and a double espresso, while Ronald had a glass of water.

'Don't you ever eat?'

'They didn't have any baked beans,' he said sadly.

Jayne shook her head. 'You should eat something different.'

'They keep me regular.'

'Too much information, Ronald,' said Jayne tucking into her quiche.

'What are we going to do?'

Jayne thought for a moment. 'Well, in the letters, we know that Dickens and Elizabeth Gaskell wrote to each regularly.'

'But it was only about their work.'

'She did write Christmas stories for his *Household Words* magazine. Perhaps if we read those, we might find out something.'

'I don't know, Mrs Sinclair, those are stories not evidence. You said we needed evidence, didn't you?'

Jayne was always surprised at how focussed Ronald was, refusing to be side-tracked when he researched. Unlike herself, who constantly discovered new documents to read and areas to look at, doubling or tripling her research time. These documents were often useful for background but not much else.

'No, you're right, Ronald,' she eventually said, 'it wouldn't be evidence.'

Ronald sat back in his chair, his shoulders hunched and his body limp. Around him, the normal buzz of the cafe swirled but he looked like he was in a world of his own.

'We've reached a dead end,' he said quietly. 'We'll never prove who Robert Duckworth was.'

Jayne hated seeing him this way. In less than a minute, he had gone from an enthusiastic, professional researcher to a depressed man who had given up all hope.

"We'll find something, Ronald.'

'What? It's already nearly three o'clock. The auction takes place in three and a half hours. What are we going to find in that time? His shoulders slumped even more if that was physically possible. 'I so wanted us to find out who he was Mrs Sinclair. It's almost as if I know him, I've looked at the inscription in the book that often.'

'Dickens must have known him, Ronald, to write such endearing words. You knew it was always going to be a difficult task in the little time we had. We made the assumption that Robert Duckworth lived in Manchester. But perhaps he was just visiting when Dickens came her in October 1843. After all, the name comes from thirty miles further north in Lancashire. Maybe, he knew Dickens already and travelled to Manchester to meet him at the Athenaeum?'

'I suppose you're right. But I wanted to give a lot of money to the homeless shelter, not just 15000 pounds.'

'That amount is amazing. Think how many people it can feed.'

'But 45,000 pounds can feed far more,' he said with unerring logic.

Jayne Sinclair tried to cheer him up. 'Don't forget, you've discovered an unknown first edition of *A Christmas Carol* with a dedication that nobody has even seen before.'

'Not strictly true, Mrs Sinclair. Whoever catalogued the book for the Crossley collection must have seen it. Remember the stamp on the inside. For some reason it was never transferred onto the Victorian sales catalogue when Crossley died.'

Jayne finished the last of her quiche and drained her coffee.

Ronald stood up. 'We've done as much as we can, Mrs Sinclair. Let's telephone Mr Underwood with the bad news. We'll have to tell him before the auction.'

Jayne sat there, feeling the caffeine from the coffee buzzing around her brain. For a moment, the sounds of the cafe vanished and the world became very still.

'Why did you just say, Ronald?'

The man frowned. 'I said we need to tell Michael Underwood before the auction. He'll have to let potential buyers understand we don't know the identity of Robert Duckworth.'

'No, before that, what did you say?'

Ronald's frowned deepened. 'I don't know, I was just talking.'

'You were talking about somebody not cataloguing something.'

'Yesss,' said Ronald doubtfully.

'Jayne stood up, snatching her notepad and pencils. 'I think I have an idea.'

CHAPTER FORTY-ONE

Thursday, December 19, 2019
John Rylands Library, Manchester

'Where are we going? What are we doing?'
Ronald grabbed his notebooks, trying to catch up with the genealogist as she ran out of the cafe.

'We need to find an unoccupied computer with a catalogue of the Gaskell collection.' A vague memory of something she had seen this morning had stuck in her mind.

They found a free computer in one of the rooms off the reception area. She logged on, checking the list of documents on Elizabeth Gaskell. 'I think they catalogued all the Dickens letters first as they would be more interesting to scholars.' She talked as she scrolled down through the catalogue. 'Bingo.' She finally said, pointing to the last time on the list; uncatalogued documents and letters.

'You think there could be some mention of Robert Duckworth here?'

Jayne glanced at the time. 'I don't know, but it's worth a shot. We only have just over three hours before auction, it's worth a try.'

'You forgot the Library closes at 5 pm.'

'Shit. Well, it just means we have ninety minutes. We'd better get moving.'

She submitted a request for the box of documents. 'Now we just hope our friendly archivist can help us out.'

They returned to their seats in the research room and waited.

And waited.

And waited.

The clock ticked over to 4.05. Finally, Jayne could stand it no longer. She walked over to the archivist standing beside the Issue Desk. 'Hi there, I put in a request for some uncatalogued letters and documents from the Gaskell Collection.'

'They just came up from storage, Mrs Sinclair. let me log then in and you can take them away.' The archivist quickly tapped her computer keys and handed over the large box. 'I'm afraid we haven't got round to cataloguing these letters completely yet. One of my predecessors performed a quick assessment, a document triage if you like. Most seem to be domestic letters. I'm afraid you'll have to return the box before five o' clock.'

'Thank you.'

Jayne seized the box and rushed back to her chair. She opened it and peered inside. 'There's a lot of documents. Let's work separately this time.'

They both put on their nitrile glove and began to work.

Ronald looked over his shoulder at the researchers behind him and then whispered. 'This ones just about the Easter celebrations for the Unitarian church.' He put it face down on new pile, taking another from the box.

'Her husband was the vicar I think.'

Jayne scanned her letter. 'It's from a cousin, detailing a planned visit to Plymouth Grove and how she was looking forward to seeing Elizabeth again, but not Manchester. She doesn't seem to have liked the city preferring the countryside around Knutsford. Perhaps, this has a *Cranford* connection?'

Jayne put it on face down on the read pile.

'This one mentions Dickens but only to say the writer went to see him reading from his books. The rest is just details of the furnishings of Plymouth Grove and church gossip.'

It too was placed on the read pile.

They continued working their way through all the letters.

The clock in the research room ticked on. At precisely, 4.50, a librarian came round and told them they should prepare to pack up as the research room was closing in ten minutes.

Jayne stared into the box. There were still at least forty letters to go. They would never read them all in time.

Ronald let out a little whoop of happiness. 'I've got something. It's a letter from her cousin in 1859, she's talking about the new house and says, "I am so happy my recommendation for a new maid is turning out to be far more diligent and accommodating in her work than her predecessor. It is always so rewarding when one can help a fellow Unitarian who has fallen on hard times. Please send my congratulations to Charlotte Duckworth and tell her how pleased I am that she has settled in so quickly.'

There was a loud, 'Please keep your voice down,' from behind them.

Jayne apologised and turned back to Ronald. 'That's great, at least it confirms when Charlotte Duckworth started working at the house.'

'But it still doesn't give us a link to Robert Duckworth.'

The minute hand of the clock ticked over towards the eleven.

Jayne placed the letter she was reading on to the read pile and reached for another, recognising the writing as soon as she picked it up.

'This is it,' she said softly.

'What?'

Louder. 'This is it.'

Ronald stopped reading his document and looked over her shoulder as she read the letter.

Dear Mrs Gaskell,

I have taken the liberty of sending you my latest novella. It is intended as a Christmas present for the guide you recommended during my time in Manchester, Robert Duckworth.

I wonder if I could trouble you to give it to him before Christmas if at all possible. I visited his abode on Newberry Street but I am not sure of his precise address in Manchester.

Thank you in advance.

I remain your honourable and admiring servant,

Jayne scrambled for her list of possible Duckworths. 'It's him, ' she shouted, 'we've found him, Ronald.' They hugged each other tightly.

There was another loud, 'Can you please keep your voices down, some of us are trying to work. This is a research room, not a rave,' from the young researcher sitting behind them.

CHAPTER FORTY-TWO

Thursday, December 19, 2019
Buxton Residential Home, Derbyshire

Jayne had set up her laptop so everybody could see it. Everybody in this case being Robert, Vera, Ronald and herself. They were in one of the small rooms off the main reception area in the Buxton Residential Home.

'I'm so excited,' said Vera, 'fancy one of my ancestors having something to do with Charles Dickens. When I was younger, I used to watch *A Christmas Carol* every year.

Jayne had photographed the documents with her phone and sent them to Michael Underwood.

He was over the moon with excitement. 'This is an amazing discovery, well done Mrs Sinclair.'

The clock on the wall ticked over to 6.30. The suspense was building as they waited for the website to go live.

The picture flashed twice and Michael appeared, standing behind a lectern with a gavel in his hand. 'Good evening, ladies and gentlemen, I would like to welcome you to the latest Underwood and Little auction being held online on this day, the December 19, 2019. This is a special Christmas sale of first editions discovered by our uniquely talented team of searchers.'

Ronald pointed to himself. 'Uniquely talented, that's me.'

'Shall we begin? Lot number 1 is a first edition of George Orwell's *Animal Farm.*' The image switched to a pictures of the book, showing the cover and inside pages before going to a dashboard showing the bids in pounds and US dollars.

Jayne zoned out for a moment and glanced across at Ronald staring at the screen. She had enjoyed herself in this investigation, it was good to have a partner to work with instead of researching alone. They had been a good team, complementing each other rather than competing. She'd like to work with Ronald again, but not to often. Baked beans for lunch everyday would start to wear her down.

She glanced across to Vera, holding her step-father's wrinkled hand. When she went into the Home, Jayne had to explain to her why she was investigating Vera's family history. It had spoilt the Christmas surprise and of course Jayne now wouldn't be able to finish it in time for her friend to create the wall chart, but Vera was as kind as ever.

'Never mind, love, it was a wonderful idea for a Christmas present. You take your time, and give it to me when you're ready. I'd love to see it, mind, I've often wondered who my ancestors were and where I came from. From what you've told me, looks like I'm Lancashire through and through. That makes me so chuffed.'

Robert saw her looking at Vera and winked. God, she loved that man. If anything happened to him…She quickly dismissed the thought from her mind. No use thinking like that. Just enjoy every minute, of every day you have left together.

In that moment, she decided she would go to Australia with these two lovely people in February. With a bit of luck, she might even discover some new clients there.

She zoned back in as she heard Michael Underwood speak again.

'Ladies and gentlemen, we now come to the star lot of the day. A first edition of Charles Dickens' *A Christmas Carol*. This unique book was a discovered in Manchester by one of our researchers, Ronald Welsh.'

Ronald beamed at the mention of his name.

"To those clients who registered interest in this lot, I have emailed details and documentation of the man mentioned in the inscription, Robert Duckworth. These documents prove the provenance and authenticity of this previously undiscovered first edition. Dickens mentions Robert Duckworth as his guide in Manchester in a letter to Mrs Gaskell kept at her archive in the John Rylands Library. In addition, there are biographical and family details found by our genealogical investigator, Jayne Sinclair.'

Jayne's face reddened.

'That's you, love,' said Vera.

'Mr Duckworth still has family living in the North of England. A connection to *A Christmas Carol* reaching back into the Victorian era when the novella was written. Anyway, without any further ado, I'd like to start the bidding at 40,000 pounds.'

The dashboard showed the bids in two currencies.

'Fancy that, so much money for a book.'

'One that used to owned by one of your ancestors, Vera,' said Robert.

'Could do with the money now, couldn't we?'

'42,000.'

'44,000.'

'46,000.'

Michael Underwood's voice came through loud and clear as the numbers on the dashboard changed.

'50,000. A bid from America. Can I see 55,000 thousand?'

The dashboard clicked over again, followed immediately by the numbers moving up to 60,000.

'Another bid from America. 65,000 anybody?'

There dashboard moved quickly to 70,000 and then 75,000.

'All this money for a book, Vera, it's amazing, isn't it?' said Robert. Vera just nodded her head transfixed by the numbers on the dashboard.

They changed to 78,000 as Michael Underwood spoke again. 'Another bid online. The book is now going for 78,000. 80,000 anybody?'

This time there was no reaction on the dashboard.

'80, 000 anybody?' he repeated, 'No, then at 78,000, the first edition of A Christmas Carol is going once, going twice, sold.'

Jayne, Vera and Robert all clapped, only Ronald looked gloomy.

'It didn't make 90,000 pounds. I was so looking forward to giving the homeless 45,000.'

Jayne put her arm around his shoulders. 'Think of it this way, you can give them nearly 40,000 and it's far more than they have at the moment.'

'I'm sure it will be a great help to tide them over after Christmas,' said Robert. 'We're just sorry we won't be here.'

As they continued talking, Jayne heard the sound of a message on her mobile phone. She searched for her bag, and dug it out.

The message was from Tom Smithson.

Dear Mrs Sinclair, I'd just thought I'd let you know, I put together a consortium of friends and we managed to purchase the first edition of *A Christmas Carol*. We were lucky though, our ceiling was 80,000.

Jayne immediately texted back.

Great news, Tom, well done to you. I'm so happy it's staying in the country where it was written.

Jayne looked up from her phone to find her Robert, Vera and Ronald still talking about Christmas.

'I'm so looking forward to telling my Scottish cousins about your book, Ronald.'

A slow smile developed on Ronald's face. 'My book? I suppose it is my book, I discovered it after all.'

'I also have something to say. We talked about it in the car driving here. Ronald and I will be spending Christmas Day together.'

Everybody looked at her including Ronald.

'And we won't be having baked beans,' she added.

His face fell. 'A great pity,' he whispered but then another broad smile spread across it. 'Just joking. I love turkey too.'

Jayne pointed to a copy of A Christmas Carol lying next to her on the table. 'We've decided to take Charles Dickens advice.'

CHAPTER FORTY-THREE

Christmas Day, 1843
Devonshire Terrace, London

Charles Dickens patted the bulging stomach beneath his gold waistcoat and pushed back his chair from the table.

They had all eaten well and celebrated even better.

He had performed his magic tricks with the help of his friend, Forster, amazing everybody with their dexterity for one whole hour. Ladies handkerchiefs had been changed into bonbons, and a box of bran had been transformed into a live guinea pig which proceeded to scurry across the table, diving into Fanny's lap.

The piece de resistance however, was pouring flour, raw eggs, raising nuts, sugar and assorted dried fruit, into a top hat, bringing out, after the correct mumbling of the magic words and waving of his conjurer's magic wand, a complete plum pudding, already steamed and ready to serve.

Even Doctor Sharp's mouth had dropped open at the audacity of the trick. He had examined Harry earlier and was positive he could effect a cure. It would be expensive but what was money when Harry's happiness and health were concerned?

It had been a good Christmas.

He still had his money worries, his publishers were still a problem to be solved and Chuzzlewit remained short of a satisfactory ending.

But *A Christmas Carol* had been an undoubted success. The six weeks he had spent feverishly writing the story had been well used. The book was handsomely printed and all 5000 copies had sold out, ensuring a second printing almost immediately.

It had not been the financial success he had hoped, profits from the sale amounted to a little less than 200 pounds, an amount unlikely to put much of a dent in the red ink of his finances. But as an artistic endeavour, it had been a triumph, with all the reviews being overwhelmingly positive.

It seemed he had struck a chord in the country, writing a book people wanted to read and remember. Even better, it was a book that had given people hope at this difficult time, exactly as he had planned.

For that, he was extremely grateful to the gods who decide the fate of all writers.

Fanny tapped the top of the pianoforte. 'Ladies and gentlemen, we wish to continue the evenings celebrations with a selection of carols.'

Harry was placed upright in a chair, while Charles was carried by his mother. Dickens' children; Boz, Mary and Kate joined Henry and Fanny. They all began singing in their perfect voices as the first chords rang out from the pianoforte.

> Silent night! Holy night
> All is calm, all is bright
> Round yon virgin mother and child
> Holy infant, so tender and mild,
> Sleep in heavenly peace
> Sleep in heavenly peace

Charles Dickens closed his eyes and listened to the music sung by his family.

It had been a good Christmas. A Christmas full of hope for the future.

What more could he want?

CHAPTER FORTY-FOUR

Christmas Day, 2019
Limelight Mission, Manchester

Jayne adjusted her red Santa hat, pushing it back over her head, and looked out over the hall. It was packed with every table occupied and the queue for food still getting longer.

A man's face in front of her peered out of a purple hoodie. She could just see a tousled grey beard, skin the colour of mahogany and eyes the clearest, brightness blue. He wore a soiled overcoat that looked as though he hadn't take it off for the last century.

'What would you like to eat?' Jayne asked indicating the turkey, vegetables, roast potatoes, and mash in trays in front of her.

'Everything, please,' the voice was deep and smoke laden.

Jayne began spooning out the food onto a plate. Ronald leaned over and said. 'We've run out of gravy, I'll just go and get some.'

For once, he wasn't feeling uncomfortable surrounded by a crowd of people. In fact, it seemed as if he were totally at home.

'Can I have more sprouts. I like sprouts.'

'No problem, I love them too.' The sprouts were perfectly cooked even if she said so herself. She'd made them this morning, parboiling and then finishing them off in a frying pan with butter and bacon. Perfect.

Ronald placed a jug next to her. 'Would you like gravy, Mr...?' she asked.

'It's Sunderland Tony, and I'd like lots.'

She thought she recognised the accent. 'Here you go, enjoy your meal. Next please.'

Another man shuffled in front of her handing across his plate.

She had been there since 7 am that morning, preparing, slicing, dicing and peeling the food, then helping to cook it. Now, she was serving it to her guests, the people who mattered; the homeless of Manchester, still spending days and nights on the streets even in the middle of winter.

Despite all the hard work, she was extremely happy. Looking over the people in the hall, she realised that Dickens had been right.

Christmas *was* a wonderful time of the year.

And while family and friends and gifts were important, even more crucial was giving back something to the people that had less than her.

Her life, despite its ups and downs, had been blessed. Others had been far less fortunate. Christmas was a time to help them and help each other.

Dickens had written about it nearly 180 years ago and he had been as right then as he was now.

She began spooning food on to the man's plate as a choir of children from one of the local churches came in and walked onto the stage.

After setting themselves up properly with the help of their choir master, a young girl, aged around ten, stepped forward to the microphone.

'Hello everyone, we're going to sing a few carols for you today. I hope you are all enjoying your Christmas lunch.'

As the girl stepped back and the choir began to sing 'Silent Night, Holy Night', a tear crept into the corner of Jayne's eye.

A gruff voice brought her instantly down to earth. 'Hang on, love, no sprouts, I can't stand them.'

'No worries, I'll give you more roast spuds instead."

'Ta, I like a roastie.'

Despite Vera and Robert not being with her, this was the best Christmas she had ever enjoyed.

'God bless you,' she said as the man walked away with his tray.

He stopped, looking back over his shoulder, 'God bless *us,* Jayne, one and all.' A toothless smile. 'God bless us, one and all.'

<<<<>>>>

HISTORICAL NOTE

This is a work of fiction but, as ever with Jayne Sinclair novels, it has a foundation of fact.

It came about through three serendipitous events.

The first was being given a copy of *A Christmas Carol* as a present when I was just thirteen years old. This Christmas gift was to begin a lifelong love affair with Dickens and his stories.

The second was buying an old book from a second-hand shop a couple of years ago, and discovering a book plate inside describing that the book had been given to a Miss Sarah Hardcastle by a Methodist Sunday School in 1899. Using the Census of 1901, I was able to find out who the young girl was, and follow her life until her death in 1972.

The third event was discovering by chance that Dickens visited Manchester often because his sister, Fanny, lived in the city with her husband until her untimely death in 1848. In fact, he visited the city just ten days before he began writing *A Christmas Carol.*

This all started me thinking, and I began to research the genesis of the Dickens novel.

A Christmas Carol was written in six feverish weeks starting around October 15, 1843 and ending on December 2nd of the same year, being published to high acclaim in the edition described in my book.

The fact that Manchester inspired A Christmas Carol is undoubted. He gave a speech at a fund raising event for the Manchester Athenaeum on October 5, 1843, visiting the city and spending time with his sister.

There is no mention of such a novel in his letters before his visit, nor had he described any plans to write anything about Christmas or with a Christmas theme prior to going to Manchester.

In his personal life, he was under immense financial pressure during the visit, having been just informed that he was overdrawn at his bank.

Debt and bankruptcy play a large role in Dickens' works.

The memories of his father being thrown into debtor's prison and him being sent to work in a blacking factory at the same time, haunted him for the rest of his life.

His publishers, Chapman and Hall, were not supporting him, as his latest serialisation, *Martin Chuzzlewit*, was not doing well. In fact, they were seeking money from him. He was still only half way through writing the story, and had not yet worked an ending.

This lack of support continued with *A Christmas Carol*. He ended paying for the first edition himself, commissioning the illustrator, John Leech, and choosing the paper stock and the binding himself.

To add to all these woes and pressure, his wife, Catherine, was pregnant with his fourth child and his father was in debt yet again, demanding that Dickens give him money..

All in all, it was not the most propitious time to consider writing a new book, but we are fortunate that Dickens did.

Ten days after leaving Manchester, despite everything going on in his life, he began work on *A Christmas Carol*, full of desire to get his words down on paper.

The rest, as they say, is history.

As for the cast of characters I have assembled in this novel, some are factual and others the result of my imagination.

James Crossley did collect books, founding the Chetham Society in 1843, and often collaborating with Harrison Ainsworth, a friend of Dickens.

Elizabeth Gaskell was living in Manchester at this time with her husband, a Unitarian minister. Dickens had just joined the congregation in London so it would be more than likely that he would have been introduced when he visited the city. He also played a large role in Mrs Gaskell's later career as a novelist, often advising her on her books and stories. The Gaskell collection at John Rylands Library contains many letters from Dickens to her.

Manchester was the centre of England's (and the world's) cotton industry at this period. Silas Grindley is a figment of my imagination. But he represents the Benthamite views of many of the mill owners of the time. Views repeated in one of Dickens' later novels, Hard Times, and its character, Mr Gradgrind.

Lizzie Burns is a real character. She was the daughter of an Irish cotton worker who became Friedrich Engels mistress, living with him until the 1870s while he was working at his father's mills in Eccles and Salford. Unfortunately, she left no written records of her life, but she is a fascinating character.

There are plenty of written records of the living conditions in Manchester at this time. Angel Meadow was as bad as I have described it (and probably far worse). Today, it is a park and part of the area favoured for living by the young and ineffably trendy known as Northern Quarter.

Robert Duckworth, however, is an invented character but the methods Jayne uses to search for him are valid.

The 1851 Census for Manchester did suffer water damage in London and parts of it are unreadable.

Finally, a word about the libraries featured in this book. Manchester is blessed with four amazing, world-class libraries, a function of the mill owners following Dickens advice in his speech at the Athenaeum and using their hard earned brass to create oases of civilisation amongst the mill chimneys.

Chetham's Library was founded in 1653 and is a beautiful building, well worth a visit if you are in the city. The Portico Library opened in 1806, and is still open to this day, serving a lovely lunch along with a wonderful selection of documents and books.

The John Rylands Library established by Enriqueta Rylands in 1900 is an amazing temple to learning, even enjoying a visit from the Korean girl band, Blackpink, last year.

Finally, Central Library, opened by the future Edward VIII in 1934, is where I spent a lot of time as a child, not doing much reading I'm afraid but enjoying the peace and serenity of the place. It has recently been renovated and is an indispensable source for genealogists researching their Manchester ancestors.

As ever, I will leave the last word to Dickens. He loved Christmas and his novel shows that love on every page. He believed fervently that the only way to improve the world was to rid it of want and ignorance through education. A declaration he made plain in his speech at the Athenaeum which I quote in my book. In a Christmas Carol, he is far more literary in his denunciation.

"This boy is Ignorance. This girl is Want. Beware them both, and all of their degree, but most of all beware this boy, for on his brow I see that written which is Doom, unless the writing be erased." Charles Dickens, *A Christmas Carol*

This is the essential message of A Christmas Carol, and perhaps the reason why it resonates so profoundly with people even though the book was written 176 years ago.

I'll leave the final word with Tiny Tim and wish all my readers a very, very Merry Christmas and a Happy New Year.

'God bless us, every one!'

If you enjoyed reading this Jayne Sinclair Genealogical Mystery, please consider leaving a short review on Amazon. It will help other readers know how much you enjoyed the book.

If you would like to get in touch, I can be reached at www.writermjlee.com. I look forward to hearing from you.

Other books in the Jayne Sinclair Series:

The Irish Inheritance

When an adopted American businessman who is dying of cancer asks her to investigate his background, it opens up a world of intrigue and forgotten secrets for Jayne Sinclair, genealogical investigator.
She only has two clues: a book and an old photograph. Can she find out the truth before her client dies?

The Somme Legacy

Who is the real heir to the Lappiter millions? This is the problem facing genealogical investigator Jayne Sinclair.
Her quest leads to a secret that has been buried in the trenches of World War One for over a hundred years — and a race against time to

discover the truth of the Somme Legacy.

The American Candidate

Jayne Sinclair, genealogical investigator, is tasked to research the family history of a potential candidate for the Presidency of the United States of America. A man whose grandfather had emigrated to the country seventy years before.
When the politician who commissioned the genealogical research is shot dead in front of her, Jayne is forced to flee for her life. Why was he killed? And who is trying to stop the details of the American Candidate's family past from being revealed?

The Vanished Child

What would you do if you discovered you had a brother you never knew existed?
On her deathbed, Freda Duckworth confesses to giving birth to an

illegitimate child in 1944 and placing him in a children's home. Seven years later she returned for him, but he had vanished. What happened to the child? Why did he disappear? Where did he go?
Jayne Sinclair, genealogical investigator, is faced with lies, secrets and one of the most shameful episodes in recent history as she attempts to uncover the truth. Can she find the Vanished Child?

The Silent Christmas

In a time of war, they discovered peace.
When David Wright finds a label, a silver button and a lump of old leather in a chest in the attic, it opens up a window on to the true joy of Christmas.
Jayne Sinclair, genealogical investigator, has just a few days to unravel the mystery and discover the truth of what happened on December 25, 1914.
Why did her client's great-grandfather keep these objects hidden for so long? What did they mean to

him? And will they help bring the joy of Christmas to a young boy stuck in hospital?

The Sinclair Betrayal

In the middle of a war, the first casualty is truth.
Jayne Sinclair is back and this time she's investigating her own family history.
For years, Jayne has avoided researching the past of her own family. There are just too many secrets she would prefer to stay hidden. Then she is forced to face up to the biggest secret of all; her father is still alive. Even worse, he is in prison for the cold-blooded killing of an old civil servant. A killing supposedly motivated by the betrayal and death of his mother decades before.
Was he guilty or innocent?
Was her grandmother really a spy?
And who betrayed her to the Germans?
Jayne uses all her genealogical and police skills to investigate the world of the SOE and of se-

crets hidden in the dark days of World War Two.
A world that leads her into a battle with herself, her conscience and her own family.

The Merchant's Daughter

After a DNA test, Rachel Marlowe, an actress from an aristocratic family, learns she has an African ancestor.

She has always been told her family had been in England since 1066, the time of William the Conqueror, and they have a family tree showing an unbroken line of male descendants.

Unable to discover the truth herself, she turns to Jayne Sinclair to research her past.

Which one of her forbears is Rachel's African ancestor? And, who is desperate to stop

Jayne Sinclair uncovering the truth?

Jayne digs deep into the secrets of the family, buried in the slave trade and the great sugar estates of the Caribbean.

Can she discover the truth hidden in time?

Printed in Great Britain
by Amazon

63293813R00180